A
Strange
Encounter

John Clegg

Grosvenor House
Publishing Limited

The right of John Clegg to be identified as the author of this
work has been asserted in accordance with Section 78
of the Copyright, Designs and Patents Act 1988

The book cover is copyright to John Clegg
Cover images are supplied by and copyright to Alexander Preston
(Alexandra Preston Photography, Bridgnorth, Shropshire)

This book is published by
Grosvenor House Publishing Ltd
Link House
140 The Broadway, Tolworth, Surrey, KT6 7HT.
www.grosvenorhousepublishing.co.uk

This book is a work of fiction. Any resemblance to
people or events, past or present, is purely coincidental.

A CIP record for this book
is available from the British Library

ISBN 978-1-80381-829-0
eBook ISBN 978-1-80381-830-6

Dedication

To all those with a slightly mad streak and to all those driven crazy by labyrinthine, faceless officialdom and political correctness.

Preface

I happened to be on a country walk one day and the thought struck me, 'Wouldn't it be strange if I heard a forsaken telephone ringing. If I answered the call, where would it lead?'

I returned to that question a number of times and then suddenly, for some odd reason the story just seemed to write itself, until at the end of forty days I was staring at a completed manuscript.

Needed a fair deal of correcting of course, but the essence of it was entire.

Acknowledgements

Thanks to my good friend, Ruth Macklin-Smith, a grand young girl of 94 who laughed at extracts I wanted her opinion on, as I read them over the phone.

Thanks to an old school mate, Joe Reece, whose candid honesty I tolerate when he's of a mind to be captious, for with even him saying he enjoyed the book, I knew I could be in with a chance. Plus credit where it's due; he pointed out a few minor errors I'd missed when proof reading.

Also, thanks to my cousin Jen Elkin, who read the first rough draft in two sittings and said, "John, you have to get it published."

Acknowledgments

Introduction

Well as you can imagine, a lady features quite strongly in the story and also popping up in the tale are current topics, but all, well nearly all, are dealt with in a fairly tongue in cheek, insouciant manner. The location is fictional, but if you happen to live in middle England, you might just recognise a few places I've borrowed snippets from.

Of course, I don't want to give the plot away, but must explain, when starting the tale, even I didn't know for sure where its windings would take me. All I can say is, a certain magic that was hard to comprehend, seemed to evolve between the two main characters, leaving me wondering, 'Where did that come from?' Like I said, the story seemed to write itself.

Part One

Part One

Chapter One

As I sit here writing, it's almost as if everything that has recently happened was nought but a dream. I know a good many won't believe the contents of this tale, but nonetheless, I feel compelled to record it, plus with these being my twilight years there comes a further compulsion, best make haste before they come for me. That last slow ride in the long black car.

I also find typing therapeutic, for what happened left me feeling quite bereft. How else could one describe it? Having unexpectedly been gifted the most exciting passage of one's life, joyously lifted from an existence where I no longer felt I belonged, only to then be dumped back to earth again, feeling like an empty shell. As I said, typing this short saga helps. Lifts me from a state of futility. Helps me rise above what people now accept as a normal life.

I won't go into further details of that now. First I'd better tell you how it all began.

From being quite a sporty type years ago, I had to content myself with walking, looking out for wildlife and exchanging greetings with folks along the way. With it having been dry for a while, on the day in question, I decided to venture into the woods. The canopy had turned to copper and gold and I just stood feeling quite humble as leaves floated down the shafts of sunlight. The main path ahead led out to open common ground, below to my left was the glint of a stream I always loved exploring and up to my right was a gentle slope, where nothing more than an animal trail led to where I knew not.

Strange as it sounds, it was from up in that direction I could hear a phone ringing. I smiled to myself, for I imagined an old-fashioned black receiver vibrating in its cradle above the inclined dialling wheel, as the chrome-plated bell rang. The sound, floating on the breeze was so perfectly clear, I expected to then hear a voice answering the call. But no, silence ensued.

When it rang again, I decided to investigate. It was not an arduous climb and the trail led between the trees to a small clearing. The ringing stopped and out of interest I fished my mobile from a jacket pocket and was not surprised to see there was no signal, making the whole thing seem even more bizarre.

I jumped slightly, for the ringing recommenced and walking to the far side of the clearing I saw the device lying beside a clump of ferns. Cautiously, I bent, picked it up and looked for a way to answer the call. I'm not that well up on modern technology, but could see instantly, this piece of equipment must have been cutting-edge.

I pressed the only button visible, an indented green one and said, "Hello?"

"Oh thank you so much for answering."

The timbre of the voice led me to imagine a lady of middle years.

"The dratted thing must have slipped from my pocket," she continued. "Good job I had my spare with me."

"Where exactly are you? I could walk and meet you." Then hastily added, "To give you the phone of course." Times had become so strange. I didn't want any suspicion of being some sort of stalker.

"Well I don't really know. I'm on a hill amongst a clump of trees."

"That sounds like Barker's Knoll. If you look below you to the north, can you see a stream?"

"Just a minute. Can't see a stream, but way in the distance there's a church spire."

"No, I'm afraid that's Lower Thresham to the south. Go to the other side and look down."

I could actually hear the rustle of clothes as she walked, followed by, "Oh there it is. How pretty."

"Now from what I remember, there are two paths. Take the one to the left and it leads to an old wooden bridge across the stream. I'll meet you there."

"Oh, you are kind."

The phone clicked, end of call and crossing a strange circular patch of flattened fern and grass, I eased my way back down to the main path.

It wasn't a long walk and as I stood beside the mossed bridge, I gazed up the hill expecting to see a redoubtable lady in Barbour jacket, green wellies and scarf approaching. There was no sign and so I waited, wondering where she could have got to.

The phone rang again. "You must think me silly. I've looked, but there's no sign of a bridge."

"So where are you?"

"On a broad curve of the stream and there's sheer banking far side."

"Oh, I know what you've done. You've taken the wrong path. No matter. Wait there. I'll be with you in a few minutes."

The lady was not the redoubtable county type I'd imagined, but a shapely package of medium height and although wearing a headscarf, it was more in the manner of a folk-bandana. A very lived in looking casual jacket topped a russet-coloured pullover and her tight jeans were tucked, not into wellingtons, but comfortable looking soft leather boots.

With an infectious smile, she said, "Ah, my knight in shining armour." Then with a teasing look, "I bet I know exactly what you're thinking."

"You do?"

"Yes. Typical woman, doesn't know her north from left or south from right."

She was a very attractive lady and had managed to do something most hadn't. She'd made me laugh and I was annoyed that my voice sounded rather hoarse when replying, "I don't think we're allowed to assume things to be typical anymore. There's always some prickly type seeking to be offended."

With a finger playfully reprimanding, she said, "But you were thinking it, weren't you?"

We walked downstream to the bridge and I suggested we return to town via the path far side. It could be treacherous after rain and I'd once nearly ended up flat on my back, but with it having been so dry recently, there wouldn't be a problem.

Halfway across the bridge I felt a tug on my sleeve. Her fingers were surprisingly long and refined and I was relieved to see no sign of a wedding ring.

"Stay awhile," she said. "I love watching the water. Look at its never-ending turns, with light reflecting like so many dreams."

As we lent on the rail, I told her of things I'd seen on my wanderings and how sometimes, I'd simply find a place to sit and watch, letting nature come to me, rather than the other way round. Her eyes lit up as I described seeing the iridescent flash of a kingfisher and when told of the rare sight of a salmon ghosting up to spawn, she opined, "I hope no-one caught it."

After a spell of silence, there came the pronouncement, "I bet, what would really cap it all, what you really hope to see one day, is an otter."

On the one hand, I felt wave instinctive warmth towards this woman of such empathy, but on the other, slight disquiet at how easily she'd invaded my thoughts.

"You're not a mind reader, are you?"

"I don't think anyone can actually read another's mind. Can you imagine it? The slapped faces, the animosity and tears. It's just as well at times, we don't know what others are really thinking."

As we walked along the far banking, I answered her queries regarding what I'd done in my life, but kept it brief, for I was more at pains to gently probe into her own past.

I then asked, "Aren't you concerned for your safety, walking out here alone?"

"Oh no. The people I meet seem friendly."

"But it only takes one sick nutcase. You need to vary the time you go walking."

We came to a dip where the original path had been washed away. Holding on to a loop of exposed tree root, I lowered myself, then reached up to help. Smiling, she took my hand and on slithering down the final section, said, "Ooh, that was fun."

I found out, she had worked in the diplomatic service, posted to places all over the globe. She told me of fly infested jungles, beautiful mountainous locations, parched open wastes that were so icy in winter and scorching through summer, she couldn't imagine anyone in their right mind wanting to live there. On one excursion, three had taken to alleviate the boredom of their posting, they thought they'd happened upon a surviving relic from the middle-ages, until accepting the invitation to enter the yurt. The large Mongolian family within, were splitting their sides laughing at an episode of Benny Hill on satellite TV.

Her anecdotes made my life seem dull and I noticed, none strayed into the convolutions of politics or the regimes she'd had to deal with. My one clumsy probe brought a distant stare, before she brightly said, "Look! I just saw a fox!"

I hadn't noticed it myself, but said, I occasionally caught sight of them and that I knew of a place where badgers could be seen in the evening.

"Oh, could you take me there?"

"We'd need to get there just before dusk. Pity you weren't here in May. The cubs were a joy to watch, chasing each other around and up and down the banking."

From that point on, I made a decision, if ever we met again, never to probe into the political workings of her former job, reasoning, she was probably still under an oath of secrecy, but I did say, "They must have let you retire incredibly early."

With a wicked grin she replied, "You old charmer."

'Here, less of the old,' I thought to myself.

Back at the edge of town our paths diverged and my offer to walk her home was politely refused, but she did say she would like us to meet again. "At *our* bridge," she chortled, obviously enjoying her touch of melodrama, regarding our chance encounter.

"But when? And I don't know your name."

"Just let it happen. Call me Helena."

I walked the short distance to my house, feeling a warm inner glow, but chided myself at not having pinned her down to a definite rendezvous. 'Call me Helena,' I mused. What an enigmatic lady.

Chapter Two

The following day the dry spell ended and watching the rain lancing down and hunched figures battling forward beneath brollies, I decided I was staying put. No point in going anywhere.

The next day was dark and dismal until about 4pm and I was just contemplating a stroll in the pallid sunlight, when my phone rang. I nearly dropped the thing. It was Helena.

"Yes fantastic," I replied to her query, but the woods will be too wet and muddy. "How on earth did you know my phone number, by the way?"

"I don't. My phone does."

"How can it? That's not meant to be possible."

"Don't ask me. It does the strangest things. Quite beyond me. I just need to add your name so I can find you again."

"Call me Daniel," I said and she laughed.

We met at the park gates and on the stroll towards the lake, I explained where I lived, stressing the fact it was only very---I used the word modest rather than basic.

She simply shrugged and asked, "If it's not an impertinence, could I visit one day?"

Of course, I was delighted by the prospect and said I'd cook her a meal, but any attempt at gently teasing out the location of her abode, was met by a blank look and an incredible adroitness at changing the subject.

Pointing to a plump, grey haired figure by the lake, she said, "Look, that old dear's feeding the ducks."

The birds, gliding effortlessly towards her, had an air of serenity until reaching the scattered bread, where they squabbled and splashed in a most fractious clatter.

I felt my arm being squeezed as Helena said, "Aren't they funny."

From a nearby bench came a doom-laden pronouncement. "You know you shouldn't be feeding them."

The woman, slowly straightening, turned and said, "You wha?"

The man stiffening his posture, said haughtily, "It's against the rules."

"Is tha' all you got?" The woman demanded, stressing each word in disgust. From her accent, she'd almost certainly originated from the east end of London.

"Whatever do you mean, madam?"

"You 'eard me. Is tha' all you got?"

"I'm not certain I understand."

"Look! If that's all you got to worry abaht, I bloody-well feel sorry for ya!"

Scrunching up the paper bag and meaningfully throwing it in a bin, she shuffled off around the lake shore.

Helena, said laughing, "I like being with you. You make things happen. Foxes, funny old ladies."

I smiled, but had to check my emotions. Helena was years my junior and I felt in danger of becoming a silly old fool, especially as she had seemed to have taken the very words, 'You make things happen,' straight out of my mouth.

Chapter Three

Two days on from this, prospects looked bright enough for a walk and so having met at *our* bridge we walked up to the summit of Barker's Knoll. Helena wore black leggings and a belted knitwear top, long enough to act as a short skirt. The coat that topped all was of a metallic looking light-weight fabric I didn't recognise.

I commented on how unusual it seemed and she replied it was waterproof and surprisingly warm. "In fact, I think I'll have to take it off. Here, feel the texture. No not the outside. Feel the underside."

She laughed at my look of puzzlement, "It feels like the warmest fur."

At the summit, the full extent of the breeze buffeted and she spread it out for us to sit on. I had also removed my coat on the ascent and draped it around our shoulders.

"Nice and cosy," she said snuggling closer. Then with a peel of laughter, "You smell like stew!"

My halting reply, that I shouldn't have worn my pullover while preparing the previous evening's meal, seemed to make matters worse and I looked on helplessly while she rocked with laughter.

Once a little calmer I enquired, where exactly had she obtained her strange coat? I sensed a marketing opportunity, but she simply took on that far-away stare I'd noticed on a previous occasion, before suddenly pointing to say, "Look at those shadows. As the clouds sail on, the sun lights up patches like little worlds that weren't visible before. Look, there's a pool I hadn't noticed. Now there's the silver sparkle from a stream, like a pretty thread of necklace."

I told her I often watched the changing shapes, like huge white galleons passing overhead and that apparently no two cloud formations are ever exactly the same. I went on to explain that each billowing cumulus held the weight of water equal to that of a massive herd of elephants or a school of blue whales.

"How do they all stay up there?" she asked looking puzzled.

"I really don't know. I suppose the water vapour rises on the thermals and somehow just stays there until the clouds cool and it starts to rain."

"Fascinating," she said gazing upwards. "You know some amazing things."

"It's not amazing really. I just take an interest in certain subjects."

Snuggling closer, she asked with a look of devilment, "So tell me. Which exactly are the elephants and which are the whales?"

Hearing my resigned sigh, she apologised for teasing, then said, pointing again, "Look, there's a perfect hole straight through that puffy-mountain cloud."

"Yes, just a fleeting aperture to the sky beyond."

"When cloud watching, you sometimes wish, don't you."

"We all wish, but some more than others. Anyway, wish what exactly?"

Peering up at the unusual formation, she asked, "How often have you seen such a perfect tunnel through the clouds?"

Thinking about it, I said, "Not often. Why?"

"Well I'm guessing you've held a secret wish, of wanting to fly like a plane, straight through to the clear blue yonder."

I remember being so completely stunned, it was to the point of feeling quite vulnerable, for it was as if she could actually see inside my head.

With the cloud pattern slowly shifting, we sat in silence, gazing at the changing colours of the tapestry below and I have to admit, even though having reached a certain level of seniority, it's still almost impossible to prevent the odd improbable romantic notion from rising to the surface. Perhaps, with men being such poor deluded creatures, there's no way of helping it. We just happen to be born like it.

Anyway, the remark, "That stewy smell doesn't seem so strong now," put paid to any such fantasies and when she added perhaps the breeze had blown it away, I answered with yet another resigned sigh, that no, she had simply got used to it.

Helena did hold my hand on the steepest slopes of the descent, which brought a touch of comfort.

We parted as before on the edge of town and I decided not to pursue her company further. Not immediately, anyway. The last thing I wanted was to create the impression of being a sad old recluse, desperately in need of female company. Besides, her ability at times, to pinpoint exactly what I was thinking was quite unnerving. A poor old soul such as I, didn't want to become a plaything, a figure of fun. No, I would keep my distance.

However, two days later, when the phone rang, I somehow knew it was her and almost dropped the thing, fumbling to answer. Seeing the name Helena beckoning was like a siren's call, but my finger must have been wet, for attempts to swipe the screen simply left smudges. A final angry stab proved useless and the annoying jingle finally stopped.

I rang her back, "Sorry, Helena, this phone of mine is that annoying I could throw it at the wall sometimes."

"Have you been running? You sound out of breath."

Out of breath? My heart was pounding that hard I'm surprised she couldn't hear it. "Nice of you to ring, Helena. What a pleasant surprise."

"You mentioned badger watching. I thought it might be nice to venture out this evening."

I was on the point of suggesting she call round for something to eat first, a light snack, not stew, but then thought it sounded too keen and so said I would call and pick her up.

"But you don't know where I live."

"I know, but I would if you told me."

"No, I'll tell you what,--- we'll meet somewhere."

I suggested the path leading to the woods and said I'd be there at 4.30. The badger sett was actually directly above the old mossed bridge we'd dallied at, but there was no way I wanted her walking there alone.

I made sure I was there ahead of time and stood waiting. It was quite chilly and more like a time to be heading for the warmth of home rather than tramping around in dank woods. A figure did approach, but it was a man walking his dog. It shouldn't be considered that strange for a person to be standing in the dusk alone, but the dogwalker gave me a suspicious look and when his hound shaped up to give the base of the lamppost a squirt, he hauled it away. The dog looked back at me accusingly.

A light tap on the shoulder made me jump. It was Helena, not emerging from town as expected, but the woods. I gave her a kiss on the cheek and was repeating my concerns about what danger she could be risking wandering out alone at night, when her, "Please don't make a fuss, darling," left me open mouthed.

She wore the dark coat as before, black leather boots and on her head was a rather fetching mink-fur hat, completing such a neat package, one could almost imagine plucking her up, for placing on the nearby picnic table for admiration. I remember thinking at the time, not even this perceptive little madam could guess such wild imaginings, but when she glanced up, pretty face framed by dark locks, I swear there was a glint of knowing in the smile she flashed.

We crossed the stream and I led the way up to the badger sett, praying they would appear. I remember thinking at the time, 'I've the good fortune to have in my company, a lady who could turn heads in the theatre, or opera house and what am I doing? Leading her up into a damp muddy tangle.' I did plod on of course, but each step increased the embarrassment at feeling so clumsily parochial.

There was enough light remaining to find the right vantage spot and on seeing the bin liners I'd brought to sit on, Helena said, "How thoughtful," before daintily snuggling up beside me. We waited, hunched in the cold. An owl hoot would have been welcome or the rasping yap from a vixen, but no, this wasn't a film set and we remained there in a yawning silence.

The chill was beginning to get into my bones and as hushed as possible, I blew on my fingers. The moon had risen, its halo heralding a frost and attempting to hurry things on, I opened the tin of cat food I'd brought as a lure and using a twig, deposited the contents in three dollops along the bottom of the banking.

Still we waited and with tension mounting I felt a compulsion to apologise profusely, abandon the venture and hurry Helena back to civilisation, for a bit of warmth in a cosy lounge bar or restaurant.

Suddenly, I felt my sleeve being gripped.

She had seen a nose sniffing the air and we watched as the black and white striped creature emerged from the banking opposite. Soon, other murky shapes followed to start snuffling about.

Whispering, I pointed out the two cubs. They were now almost the size of their parents and although making as if to chase one another, it was only half-hearted and going their separate ways, looked more interested in rooting out food.

Again, I felt my arm being squeezed. The badgers had found the gift I'd left and were noisily guzzling. Once satisfied only the aroma remained, they made their way off into the undergrowth.

Folding up the bin bags, we left the creatures in peace and Helena, allowing me to take her hand, followed as we carefully picked our way back down to the stream.

Standing together on the bridge, I expected a teasing comment, such as, "Well! You certainly know how to show a girl a good time," but no, she said, "That was quite magical, thank you."

"Back in May, there were three cubs, but one must have been run over or simply starved to death."

"What do they eat?"

"Any small creature they chance upon, but spend most of their time digging up earthworms."

"What, big things like that eat worms?"

"I know it seems strange, but they do. Much of their liquid intake comes from them."

Helena, pulling a face, said, "Yuk."

"They're also partial to wasp grubs. I've seen a whole nest ripped out from a stretch of banking."

"Surely they'd get stung to death."

"Not at night."

The stream below played its gentle music and concerned Helena might be getting chilled, I suggested we return home.

"No don't go yet. The stars are so beautiful. Do you ever feel like they're calling you?"

Standing there, still holding the empty food tin and a frost descending, I have to be perfectly honest, I felt like saying, 'No, quite frankly I've never felt drawn to them in that way,' but with her face staring up in such wonder, I of course didn't. Instead, I confessed, that other than being able to pick out the obvious, like the Plough, I knew little about them.

"Well I don't really," she replied, "but if you look over there you'll see Aquarius, Capricorn and Sagittarius. Oh, and you can just see the planet Jupiter." She pointed again and bubbling with enthusiasm, added, "Follow this line," and slowly tracing with a finger, she said, "Aquila, Lyra, Vego and Draco."

"How do you know all this? I wouldn't even know how to find the North Star."

"Oh, Polaris. You'll need to look over there to the north west. Can you see the Plough?"

"Yes. As I said, it's one shape I do recognise."

"If you look at the two outermost stars on the edge of what looks like a ladle and go directly north---"

"You mean, to that bright star?"

"Yes, you've found it. That's Polaris."

"What about the famed Orion's Belt."

"We'll have to come back after Christmas," she said with a laugh.

As we walked back to town I mused over the fact, that this lady who knew her way around the stars and exactly where north west was, had supposedly not known left from right or north from south, on our first meeting.

Apparently, with little else to take up the time at night, all this knowledge had been picked up on foreign postings.

Yet again, I felt frustration at her not allowing me to walk her home, but at least she suggested we meet again soon. Then on gazing up at me and avowing she thoroughly enjoyed our little outings, Helena stood on tiptoe to plant a cool, open-lipped kiss on my cheek and leaving perfume's sweet redolence lingering, headed off down the street.

Still holding a smelly tin, I called out in jest, "I'll not be washing my face tonight," which brought a sway of hips along with the backward wave of understanding.

Chapter Four

We didn't see each other for a while, as one of those Atlantic storms had blown in wreaking havoc. I limited my outings to buying food, including dropping off a few necessities for a lady living in the same street, who had problems getting about.

Helena and I kept in contact by phone and when the weather calmed, I suggested a trip into town. It was the first time I'd seen her in high heels, which gave a pert lift to her all-enveloping cashmere coat. Glint of gold beneath tresses, red lipstick and a smile were enough to send a rush of blood through my system, a frisson immediately quashed by our boarding of the town bus.

As I paid, I heard a sarcastic, "Ooh, so we're to be graced with lady's company," which was the reason I plumped for the two seats recently alighting passengers had left near the front. I was embarrassed enough already without blundering my way to the back, with Helena having to suffer being the centre of attention. We weren't sitting together, but were only going a couple of stops. I silently cursed, 'Why hadn't I driven, or ordered a taxi?' Feeling like a bumbling old fool, I tried to console myself with, 'How was I meant to know she would turn up as if suddenly springing from a fashion magazine?'

To make things worse, the woman beside me, said, "Excuse me, but would you mind swapping, so my friend can come and sit next to me."

"Not really a problem," I said, "but I'm only going as far as the Royal."

"Oh, it doesn't matter then. Sorry to be a nuisance."

Calming a little I said, "No I insist, give your friend a wave. Tell her she can have this seat. It's really not a problem."

By the time the friend had understood, the bus was sweeping in towards the next stop.

Stomping aboard, came a man of generous girth wearing a grimy mac, slightly shorter than his flowery frock and having shown his pass, he came barrelling up to plonk himself in the seat I'd just vacated.

"Excuse me," I said, "but the seat is reserved for this lady's friend to sit in."

"Tough! I've as much right to it as anyone."

All within earshot looked thoroughly disgruntled, but no-one dared say a word until the friend in question jabbed him on the shoulder and said, "Now just a minute!"

"And you can fuck off!" he snarled.

"How dare you speak to a lady like that," said I, to which he replied, "Why not. I happen to be a lady myself and so can talk to her, exactly how I like."

"Huh, in those shoes! You must be joking!" said the woman I'd vacated my seat for.

The bus had pulled into our stop and I beckoned Helena to squeeze past the altercation and wait for the door to swish open.

From behind we heard the roar of, "What's wrong with my shoes? That's a fuckin' hate crime you bitch!"

We were out on the pavement when we heard the reply. "Call yourself a lady! Ugly sister more like! Can't get Cinders' shoes to fit, so you ram yer feet into those old bunion boats!"

Helena, glancing up, looked horrified at the drama unfolding within; the raised shoe, its heal threatening a woman's face; a man's roar of, "Back off you fuckin' Karen, unless you want that ugly mug rearranged!" Then the soft snarl of an engine, as the little spectacle was transported from view.

"Well!" she said, looking quite shaken. "Things really do seem to happen when I'm with you."

"I'm really sorry about that."

"Well it was hardly your fault."

It wasn't a long walk to the Royal and I was quite keen to get there, but just as luck would have it, a jeweller's window beckoned. Helena was pointing out a gold bracelet she quite liked, when a police car, siren wailing, went absolutely hurtling down the street. People stood and stared and as we entered the shop, another followed, light strobing.

"Goodness!" said Helena.

"Must be a bank robbery," I posited.

The man in the shop was very obliging and no bracelet could have looked prettier on a slender wrist, but no, it was laid aside and alternatives tried, but in the end, it was back to the initial choice for a further try on. I murmured, "I'd love to buy it for you," which was ignored and pert as you like, Helena smiled and said, "I'd like to think about it."

The jeweller gave, what must have been a much-practiced gracious smile and we left the shop.

In the Royal, luncheon was already being served, but on Helena saying, 'Just a drink will do,' I ordered her the rather quaint choice of pink gin, plus a glass of red wine for myself. There were seats available, but I bowed to her preference of standing beside a column, where we could rest our glasses on a shelf. Obviously, we wouldn't be lingering.

With her coat now undone, I could see she was wearing a pretty, light-mauve top above a black skirt, which looking as if tailored to show off the curve of her hips, finished just below the knee. Standing with feet planted slightly apart, shapely ankles enhanced by the straps of her shoes, she gave a me measured look.

My face must have conveyed, a 'caught in the act' sort of sheepishness, for accompanying a sigh, came the resigned smile, typical of such enchanting creatures, when born with innate knowledge of what most men would be thinking.

We both turned, at the sight of three men hurrying in to join others at the bar.

"You'll never guess what's just happened," said one. "That racket earlier, was the plods arresting some geezer."

Of course, they all wanted to know why and he said, "All hell broke loose. Apparently, a bloke in a frock attacked some woman called Karen, on the town bus."

"Why, what had she done?"

"She'd taken the piss out of his shoes."

There was general laughter and shaking of heads in disbelief.

"You couldn't make it up," said one.

"Was she hurt?" asked another.

"No what happened was, this other bloke stands up, to give the bloke in the frock a bollocking and when he comes at him waving a shoe, he knees him right in the crutch."

More laughter was followed by, "Apparently the bus driver, hears all the commotion, spots a copper and pulls over to ask him to sort it out."

"Lucky to find a copper these days."

"Unless exiting the pub carpark," came a reply.

"Or doing 50 up a wide-open road, to be told there's a speed limit," said another.

"So did he arrest the bloke in the frock?" was asked with some urgency.

"You must be joking! No, not a bit of it. He bends down to gently enquire of the stricken passenger ------

"You're making it up!"

No I'm not, listen! Apparently, the bloke in the recovery position whimpers, "That nasty man kneed me!"

"Where?" asks the copper.

"Right in the nuts," says this bloke in the frock. To which, this piece called Karen pipes up, "Well if you're truly a woman you shouldn't have any!"

Once the laughter had calmed, he followed it with, "Well as you can imagine, the whole bus full cheers, but when those other plods come screaming up, all three got taken down the nick to sort it out."

One of his friends surmised, "So, I bet, Karen, or whoever she is, gets done for hate crime, the bloke that rescued her gets done for assault and the bloke in the frock gets given a mug of tea and some ice-cubes."

They were still debating the possibilities when we left the hotel.

Out on the street, Helena asked, "Why didn't the driver sort the problem out when it all started? If we could hear it, he must have done."

"Probably in fear of losing his job."

"Why?"

"You daren't say anything to men wearing frocks, these days."

"What a strange world you live in."

"What do you mean, I live in?"

There came that strange, split-second face freeze I'd seen before, followed by, "Would you really have bought me that bracelet?"

"Of course."

"You are sweet."

That word 'sweet,' hit like a silencing dart.

Chapter Five

The following meeting with Helena, again involved public transport, but having been forewarned a little walking would be involved, she arrived with hair loosely pinned and donning the casual country garb as seen on our first meeting.

I paid for our tickets using one of those confounding machines found on platforms these days. Being of advanced years is not a thing to be envied, but at least I'd been fortunate enough to have travelled when a train ride had felt romantic, exciting. Accompanied by parents, the expectation built as you approached the station and there in the entrance hall was the man behind the hatch dispensing tickets and answering queries. You would almost jig with excitement, that it wasn't just a dream, you really were catching a train that day. Really embarking on an adventure.

Outside would come the rumble of iron across stone as a laden porter's trolley was heaved along the platform. Far side of the tracks, either side of a waiting room, the gardens were a joy to behold and on seeing you, a bundle of contained excitement, your mum would warn, not to get too close to the platform edge, or to go running about where it was slippery.

Now, automated Tannoy announcements take the place of common sense, plus there's the regular assault of, "See it, say it, sorted,' annoyance.

We were told, our train was imminent, where it would be stopping and how many coaches it comprised of and nobody could complain about that, but all now seems so soulless, graffiti ravaged and bleak. Dragged down and abandoned to the level of the gutter, where people just shrug and say, "What can you do? It's what you've got to put up with these days." In other words, 'Stop moaning and get on with it, like we do.'

Oh for the sight of billowing smoke puffing above the trees, heralding the approach of a steam train; it's slowing rotation of pistons and quivering of monster's might; then the hissing; the deep panting, awaiting that spur into action again. Even the sight of a grubby little tank engine, merrily clanking while shunting trucks, could root a small boy to the spot, but you can't halt progress.

Suddenly, a group of scantily clad young women invaded our peace, tumbling in from the adjoining carriage as if discovering the funniest scream of an experience ever had in their lives.

One screeched, "It's so----" She could hardly talk for laughing. "It's so---It's so----I'm like,---- oh my GOD!"

"What are they all laughing about?" Helena asked. "I can't understand what they're saying."

"They're probably all high on those popper things," I surmised. "And as far as I can work out, they're not actually saying anything."

At this point, the door, far end of carriage slid open again and a neatly uniformed ticket inspector entered the drama. "Excuse me please, ladies."

"You've already seen ours, you creep," said one of the girls.

"I'm not asking to see your tickets, I'm simply asking to be allowed to pass."

With them blocking the aisle, he had no choice other than to carefully edge past.

"Don't you dare touch me you little perv!"

"Did he touch you? He wants reporting!"

A man sitting nearby said, "Now don't be ridiculous, the man is simply trying to do his job."

"What's it got to do with you? You fuckin' BOF!"

With this, all the girls went into hysterics, repeating, "BOF, BOF, BOF!" Like a demented pack of bitches.

"Oh my God----, think I've just wet them," said one, clutching her groin.

"You're so funny!" said another, to the instigator of such hilarity.

"But he is though. Just look at him!"

"I know. A typical BOF."

This set them all off again, but the ticket inspector did manage to continue down the carriage and Helena asked, "What did she mean? What is a BOF."

"Oh, I don't know. Probably the latest acronym." Thinking for a while I said, "It probably means something like, boring old fart."

"I'm surprised their parents let them go out dressed like that. You could hardly call it a warm day."

"It's become almost commonplace. I'm surprised you've not come across it before."

"You forget, I've spent most of my time out of the country."

I explained, "These girls dress themselves according to the part they're playing. They spend much of their lives as if on a reality TV show."

What was meant to be a pleasant day out was turning into a nightmare.

It came as a great relief, for when finally wandering the narrow streets of our destination, I saw its charm had begun to work its magic. Helena seemed entranced by the small church, the lanes with their half-timbered buildings, then as if by magic, while picking our way amongst the scant remains of the monastery down by the lake, we were bathed in sunlight.

At the tearooms, even though visiting no more than four times a year, I was cheered to be remembered and greeted like a regular. I found us a table for two and when up at the counter asking for my usual scone with homemade jam and cream, the proprietor enquired, "What about your daughter? Can't we tempt her with a little something."

"Actually, she is not my daughter. and has simply asked for an espresso coffee."

"Oh, I am sorry. I didn't mean to---"

"Don't worry. I'm sure she'll be quite amused and flattered when I tell her. By the way, I'll just have a regular coffee with the scone, thank you."

As predicted, Helena was quite tickled, but it was disconcerting that she never seemed to eat anything.

Not as disconcerting as what happened when we left, mind you. Two black Labradors had been left tethered to the rings provided and lay patiently waiting. Then, I don't know why, but the instant they caught sight of Helena, they went into such a hysterical, teeth-baring cacophony, their owner rushed out to calm them.

"I'm so sorry," he said. "I've never known them act like this before."

The animals ceased their barking, but eying Helena warily, snarled throatily with hackles raised.

As we walked away, I said, "How strange."

"Brutes like that ought to be locked up," was all Helena said on the matter.

Chapter Six

One of the best things about the Royal Hotel is that it hasn't lost its old-world charm. Beyond the main reception area and lounge bar, there's a room for patrons to sit in comfort and read the paper. It's a pleasure to have morning coffee there and in the summer, becomes that popular, one needs to book a table if wishing to take afternoon tea.

On the particular Saturday morning, Helena and I happened to pop in for a coffee, we were fortunate enough to arrive just as four were leaving, allowing us to sit in one of the most favoured spots, over by the tall windows that admit the morning sun. I hung Helena's cashmere coat on the bentwood hallstand near the door and ordered coffee.

The place was quite full, but there was an air of peace. Many were reading the papers provided, a few worked on their laptops and even the six teenagers in the corner opposite, lounged quietly. In fact they were so uncommonly quiet, Helena commented on how strange it was that none were talking, for all were engrossed on their phones. There was an occasional nudge and lean towards a friend to share something interesting, but generally it was complete absorption with phone content.

"It seems that people have never been so well connected and yet are so far apart," I said.

Our coffee arrived accompanied by those fiddley little biscuits that disintegrate in the attempt to rip open the cellophane. Helena slid her two across in my direction.

I asked if she would care to read a newspaper, but she declined, saying she'd probably only get annoyed. "From my experiences abroad, I've never read an account pertaining to my location, that hasn't made me want to fling the thing across the room. They rarely get to the truth, being content to give their readers what they think will satisfy pre-formed opinions."

"But there's still some investigative journalism."

"Only on matters that will hit the right chord. They rarely delve into contentious issues where the revelation will hit their followers with home truths. Ruffle too many feathers. Lose them readership."

Helena was actually preaching to the converted, for there were a couple of very important current issues that the media was ignoring, but it was a pleasant morning in a lovely setting and I didn't wish to upset it.

At that point, four men, probably in their late thirties, dressed in casual designer attire, breezed into the room. They exuded affluence and confidence, to the extent I wished I'd taken the trouble to polish my old worn shoes before leaving that morning. One obviously revelled in being the raconteur, with the other three content to be sycophants.

I tried talking to Helena, but my words seemed to fall on the carpet as the man's voice boomed. I leant closer, but she winced, as if the struggle to hear above his racket was giving her a headache. The country clad Helena would have probably found the whole thing hilarious, but this was cashmere coated, brittle Helena and the air around almost bristled as if energy charged.

In the end I said, "Look, I've had enough of this," but strangely, she then raised a hand for silence.

After a few minutes, sitting perfectly upright as if tuning in, she said, "He's telling them about Hong Kong. I know the street he's talking about. Bars full of carousing bankers."

"I've only been there once and that was enough. Loved the harbour ferries, mind you."

"So no doubt you know the district he's now talking about."

"No, all I can hear is a booming echo, but I suspect he's moved location down to Wan Chai."

"Lockhart road to be exact."

"What, you've been there?"

"Of course. It's totally different during the day. But obviously yours was nighttime visit."

"Yes. I was quite underwhelmed in fact. They all seemed to be very ordinary looking Filipino cleaners making a bit of money on the side."

Seeing her narrowing of eyes, as if carefully assessing the extent of my involvement, I quickly added, "And many other positions I shouldn't wonder."

A hint of a smile crept, before she pronounced, "He really is a loud-mouthed creep!"

I left money for coffee, plus a small tip on the table and we rose to leave. On fetching Helena's coat, I apologised and said it would make sense if I quickly availed myself of the facilities. At my age, especially with chance of a cool autumn breeze, I never pass up an opportunity. I noticed the four self-satisfied young men were also making a move. Helena waited by the door, with the coat draped over an arm.

Nothing could have prepared me for the scene on my return. Helena was still patiently waiting, but the swaggerer was flat on his back, with his friends looking down, open mouthed in shock.

As we entered the foyer, I heard the stricken man complaining, "I only touched her bum."

"You went down like you'd been tasered," said one of his pals.

Helena almost seemed to sail across the reception area and catching her up, I muttered, "Whatever happened?"

"Nothing more than a mild stroke," was said with a dismissive shrug.

"Just as well he never went for it with both hands then"

Country Helena, would have gone into a fit of giggles at this, but helping her into the cashmere coat, I merely received a patient smile to indicate the little quip had not gone unnoticed.

We were heading for the park once more, but to a different section, one that had a decorative a pool, rather than a lake, plus there was a bandstand and in summer, a small electric railway operated. All the various kiosks would be closed and there certainly wouldn't be any musical entertainment, but on a fine day it was still a pleasant place to stroll.

I decided to take a short cut through the once much-heralded shopping mall. I shouldn't have. Most shops were boarded up, litter was strewn everywhere, a stench of urine assaulted the nostrils and in one doorway, a poor unfortunate lay curled up asleep.

"What's happened?" Helena asked. "It's like the third world."

"I know, really depressing. I hadn't realised how far the place has sunk. But now I stop to think about it, I've not been here in months, maybe even years. I do most of my shopping in the weekly market."

We could hear skateboards rattling down one of the arteries. From the depths of another came the sound of a guitar accompanied by the melodic strain you'd expect from a rusty tin can, singing along with the chord thrashing as if venting suppressed anger. There was not the slightest chance of financial gain and so I can only imagine he was availing himself of the acoustics.

The sudden bright sunlight on emerging and broad vista of the park ahead brought a sense of freedom from the labyrinth, where the agonies still resonated in the depths and I made up my mind to ring a taxi for the return journey. We walked for a while and then sat on one of the benches down by the bandstand.

I gently probed further into Helena's background, for it was fascinating and seeing her come alive when recounting amusing anecdotes, transported me along with her story, into another world, but eventually, I plucked up courage to ask the question I probably wasn't going to like the answer to, "Why me?"

"You answered the phone that day. Simple as that."

"That was a while back. Don't get me wrong, I really enjoy our little outings, love them in fact, but there's no denying I'm much older than you, which makes me wonder, where are your friends? Those your own age?"

"You don't get it, do you."

"No, don't suppose I do."

Helena, staring at me, composed herself. "Tell me," she asked at last, "when did you first really know yourself?"

"What, the person I am today?"

"Yes."

"Mid-thirties I suppose."

"And were you happy with that person?"

"There are certain things I wished I hadn't done, but yes, basically I felt at ease with what I'd become."

"And this person, was he the same as all those others around?"

"I used to think so, but gradually it dawned on me, no I was different."

"Better?"

"Better than the rest? No certainly not. It takes all sorts, road sweepers, doctors, lords, laundrette ladies, teachers you know what I mean, but I treat them all the same. That's provided they warrant respect. I have no time for louts, layabouts, over educated idiots, or complete prats like the one we encountered earlier."

"This *you*, that had now become moulded, was he hampered by any fixations?"

"I think the term, back then, was hang-ups. No not really. The ones I'd had as a slightly confused youth, I'd left behind. But there was one sense of paucity, everybody must have at least one. It's part of life."

With Helena's gaze becoming uncomfortable, I found myself continuing, "One slight niggle of inadequacy...."

"Yes, go on."

"I'd obviously done quite well academically, but wished for, longed for in fact, a greater intellect. I felt as if my mind was in the foothills compared with a few I'd encountered. Some could rattle off interesting details as if having prepared for a lecture and could even quote from books read years earlier."

"Quite impressive, but these days you can research such detail in seconds."

"I know, but that can hardly be done when deep in the cut and thrust of fascinating discourse."

"But did such abilities make this select few, better people?"

"I really couldn't say. I just felt an admiration verging on envy. Not an all-consuming thing, but it still nagged occasionally."

"So, is it safe to say, you don't consider yourself to be one of the herd?"

This probe hit like a bit of a low flyer, eliciting the reply, "No, I have to admit, I don't. And don't actually wish to be."

"So, with now having reached such a venerable age, do you sometimes feel isolated, lonely?"

I didn't like the way this was going at all and so now slightly miffed, remained stubbornly mute.

Helena persisted, however. "Have you arrived at this point in life feeling burdened in any way?"

"You mean, carrying luggage?"

She smiled, knowing I had made light of an annoying trend-term, baggage and sighing patiently said, "Let's try it another way. If you had your time over again, would you do things differently?"

I thought for a while and with Helena now wearing a serene look, exuding no sense of threat, the silence was not uncomfortable. "There were two definite crossroads missed."

She actually cuddled against me and said, "Go on."

"One day I was hitch-hiking back to university and was picked up by a man slightly older than myself and instantly we hit it off as if we'd known each other all our lives. The conversation was that absorbing, it seemed as if within no time at all, we were on the outskirts of London. He'd already recounted tales regarding his destination, Cote d'Azur, with its wonderful weather and beautiful girls, but then added, he was actually on his way to help on a millionaire's yacht. They were a crew member short and he suggested, 'Why didn't I forget about university and come with him?'

"I had all my clothes in a suitcase and even my passport. I often wonder what would have happened had I accepted his offer."

"And the other time?"

"Well that's going back to school days. History was my first love, but no university would consider me, for although the exams passed were to the level required, I'd not passed an exam in a foreign language."

"What's a foreign language got to do with history?"

"Good question. It was the requirement at the time and so I was busy cramming for French O-level, hoping to escape the small town I felt trapped in, when out of the blue an offer came via the university clearing scheme. It was a humanities course and I'd be in the heart of London, which at the time was the most exciting place in the world."

"So you took the offer."

"Yes, but often wonder what would have happened, had I stayed resolute and gone for a history degree."

"You'd probably have ended up some dried-up old crud and I'd not have liked you anything like as much as I do."

"But don't you understand, my days are almost over."

"Don't be ridiculous. As they say, 'Age is just a number.'"

"Not when you've frequently got back ache, feel completely lost without glasses and sometimes even struggle to get a pair of shoes on."

"Where I'm from that won't matter."

Now we were coming to it. "Helena?"

"Yes?"

"Where exactly *are* you from?"

Her face, yet again, took on that momentary freeze, no more than you'd expect from a car's sat nav announcer, if visible when witnessing a wrong turn. Then like a light switching on, she said brightly, "I bet you yearn to be one of those scruffy academics, hidden behind piles of books in a gloomy room, high up in an ancient turret."

Then giving me a playful jab, "And I bet you sometimes wish you could put your hand up my skirt."

"Not if I'm going to get tasered."

It must have been my woeful look, for even the Cashmere coated Helena, went into convulsions, shaking with laughter as she leant against me.

Chapter Seven

The taxi, at Helena's insistence dropped me off first, then continued to where her car was parked.

Before parting I'd said, "You didn't tell me you had a car."

"You didn't ask."

Thinking for a while, I'd added, "So, that night we went badger watching, you didn't actually walk home, you walked to where your car was parked."

Raising of eyebrows and a shrug, had given a, 'maybe,' sort of reply, but other than that, she didn't actually say anything. I did receive a perfunctory peck on the cheek and then settling back like royalty in her cashmere coat, there came a gloved wave as the taxi pulled away. Men often struggle to understand women, but this one was truly mystifying.

My house seemed exceptionally chilly and bleak, with everything left, just as it had been when leaving that morning. Although of course logical, I never seemed to get used that rather forlorn reminder, I was living alone. Still wearing my coat, waiting for the heating to mellow the place, I don't know why, but my thoughts kept returning to that little 'hand up the skirt,' quip. Mulling it over I decided it wasn't just me being, shall I say, different to most; perhaps even a bit prudish, for as much as men would dearly like them to, ladies are not normally prone to suggesting such things. Well, some might, being part of a career choice and of course every generation, when growing up, had one or two that had a scrum of boys all over them in the back of the school bus in a teenage feeding frenzy, but even those usually went a bit prim on reaching full maturity. "None as sanctimonious as a reformed whore," came to mind. A classic line from a film, way back, but I couldn't remember which one.

Then came a slightly disturbing memory and I instantly knew why that quip had jarred. Not only was she thinking as a man would, Helena had also been quite familiar with Wan Chai, Hong Kong's red-light district. She can't have been a high-class hooker. 'Lightning strike me down for thinking such a thing!' but the nagging doubt kept eating away. I could feel its destructive power working and cursed my stupid retrospective jealousy. For there was no point deluding myself, no matter who Helena happened to be, or what she'd done in her life and no matter how well we seemed to gel together, ours could be nothing more than a platonic relationship.

I could hear the radiator in the front room making that faint ticking sound as water circulated and with the warmth gradually bringing comfort, another thought floated into consideration. The chauvinism of many men; not minding a thoroughly mucky woman, just so long as she doesn't happen to be his partner.

My decision not to call Helena for a while was helped by the fact, the next day I didn't feel so good. I made a quick dash to the shops to buy a few basics, but also bought oranges and a packet Beacham's powders.

I'd probably caught a mild chill down at the park and had enough experience to recognise the signs. That night I had a high temperature and with it, as often happens, came a crazy dream. It careered on in the most convoluted fashion, but I'll just give the basics.

There was quite an innocuous start for I was amongst friends, but on realising most of them were no longer alive, there crept an eerie feeling. We were in a huge building where all sorts of things were being auctioned and I suggested we nip to a nearby bar for a drink. Once in the bar, I was confronted by a red faced loud mouth and looking around could see only one of my friends remained. The stay in the pub was not pleasant and so both myself and the friend entered the street, but had to leap back onto the pavement, as an old-fashioned steam engine came clanking through. For some reason we climbed aboard one of the carriages, an open affair resembling a full-size version of the trains you see transporting holiday makers and having talked to a group of passengers for a while, I realised my friend was no longer with me.

We seemed to have reached a terminus, for all disembarked and I found myself beside a wide grey river flowing out to sea. The people I'd been talking to had disappeared and so I was now surrounded by strangers, on the wrong side of an undulating torrent and the city I had left behind, was but a misty blur, like a tiny bar chart along the horizon. Everyone seemed dull, listless and unfriendly, but then appearing amongst them, shining like an angel, I saw Helena.

She smiled, took hold of my arm and said, "What are you doing all the way out here? Follow me."

We came to a steep flight of wide stone steps leading down to a square where the throng was packed so tight, there seemed no way through. Then from behind, in a most hysterical frenzy, a pack of dogs came hurtling towards us.

"Quick, hold on to me," said Helena and we ran down the topmost steps to take off, flying just above head height of the stunned crowd below. She let me go, saying, "You now have the magic. Believe,--- you can do it alone."

Well as you can imagine, it was hard to believe, for I was flying, but then began to sink towards the throng, severely angered at the sight of one daring to rise above their grim existence. Some started to leap up, attempting to catch and drag me from the sky and others took swipes with sticks and umbrellas, but raising my knees, I flew in a sort of sitting position, bobbing along in the manner of an aerial seahorse, just out of range above them.

When I finally awoke, my sheets were soaked with sweat. In slippers, dressing gown, plus large woolly hat, I went down to make myself some tea. It was when draining the last drops, I felt it. When the rim of the mug touched my nose, it brought the tell-tale sting of a burgeoning boil. Gingerly, I felt the smooth protrusion and knew straight-away, it was going to be an absolute belter.

There was no way I would contemplate seeing Helena with such a Belisha beacon throbbing. I could imagine people coming up to give their hands a good warm. It wasn't until the fourth day that I could see it had peaked and so, without going into too much detail, I dared relieve the pressure. The third application of the forefingers later that day, produced little but blood, but then of course there was a small round scab.

I finally dared answer one of Helena's calls, apologised for radio silence and explained I was under the weather. Even though I was over the initial chill and my profile had returned to normal, I now of course couldn't go out with what looked like a massive blackhead on the side of my nose. I thought of giving it a gentle pick, but knew it would only bleed again, with the chance of it getting bigger.

I don't know why it is, but the fingers of certain females tend to itch when espying such a beauty, begging for the gentlest of squeezes. Probably dates back to Neolithic times when a daily grooming to keep their partner free from potential infection or vermin, meant he'd be fit to hunt and keep the family fed. Anway, I could imagine sitting ensconced in the Royal, having explained to Helena, I simply had a small scab on the side of my nose, but the inevitable group of ladies nearby, would be bound to tut-tut and say things like, "You'd think she'd tell him."

"Wouldn't let our Ernie go out with a blackhead like that on his snout!"

"That young woman with him,--- she must have seen it!"

"Seen it? You could hardly miss the thing!"

"The least she could do is give it a squeeze."

"If our Bob came home with a beaut like that, my fingers would be quivering to be at it!"

Then of course, Helena would ask, "What are those ladies so amused at?"

No, I decided I was not venturing out until the all-clear.

Chapter Eight

It happened to be a bright clear morning and as I looked out of the front room window, my heart skipped a beat, for Helena was walking up the path.

I quickly scooped up the used plate and mug to take to the kitchen; had a glance in the mirror; made sure all was zipped and shirt-tucked, before finally answering the knock on the door. "Helena, how wonderful."

She declined coffee and we sat for a while talking. I quickly checked on the internet, that no rain was forecast and suggested we go for a drive. I desperately needed some fresh air. I'd been festering indoors long enough. My car was a little way down the street with its resident's parking disc displayed and opening the passenger door, invited country clad Helena to take a seat. I apologised for it being nothing but a humble, well-used old motor, but she grinned as if we were embarking on some exciting adventure aboard a model of classic vintage.

Basically, however, we were heading for no more than a pleasant old-fashioned spot I knew. There was a duck pond where an ancient willow draped, a country store that specialised in local produce and if ones' mobile rang while in the pub, the landlord's finger pointing at the door, indicated, 'Take that call outside.'

He was a large man, brimming with health and the way his frame and personality dominated the bar, he looked the perfect advertisement for the food served there. With a clientele willing to drive miles to partake, I'd phoned ahead to reserve a table.

First, however, we went for a stroll.

"Helena?" I had remembered that a pronouncement said on our previous meeting had alluded to something, but the subject had been left dangling. "What exactly did you mean when you said, 'You don't get it?'"

Country clad Helena furrowed her brow as if having to rewind the tape. I almost imagined her asking, as if about a completely different person, "What exactly did that little madam tell you?" But no, having given my arm a conspiratorial squeeze, she said, "Well, cast your mind back. When you were a young man, off to a dance or party, did you ever wonder why sometimes you seemed to almost charm the birds off the trees and yet at others, no matter how hard you tried, everything you did fell flat."

"Yes, how do you know that?"

Having been given a quick peck on the cheek in encouragement, I continued, "Some nights I would turn up, virtually a gate-crasher, in clothes I'd been wearing all day and end up having a whale of a time. Then on other occasions I'd make a special effort and have no luck at all."

"And you never worked out why."

"No, not really. You won't have heard of that Gracie Fields song, you're too young, but it went, 'I brought me 'arp to a party, but no-one asked me to play.' That was how it felt sometimes, to the extent I was almost paralysed by a phobia creeping, scared to ask a pretty young thing to dance in case she said no. I remember saying to a university mate, "I like the look of those two over there, but they might be with someone.""

He said, "If we piss about much longer they will be."

Helena laughed and I added, "It seemed grossly unfair that all the onus was on the man. Believe me, it's an awful long lonely walk back after a refusal."

"Like I said, you don't get it do you? Did it never occur to you, that often the reason you were successful was because the lady liked what she saw and in actual fact, you didn't pick her, she picked you. Didn't matter you had turned up looking like a complete scruff bag, for she liked your personality. Then when you went to all that trouble, to look like Mr. Slick with hair combed, it probably acted as a turnoff. Made you look a bit unapproachable and rather dull."

"You mean, it's taken me all these years to find this out. It's a bit late now."

"You see, many ladies, on spotting untamed potential, know full well, with a bit of reshaping, the man can be transformed into a successful cutting edge, with her alongside relishing where life takes them."

"You mean, that old adage, 'Behind every successful man.....'"

"Yes, that sort of thing."

Now came a brave question. "Look Helena. I hate to ask this, but it feels rather strange us being together so often, -----have you actually picked me? If you have, I'm afraid you've left it far too late. I'm as good as past it and don't have much money."

"No money!" she said laughing. "Back to the car then. Drive me home this instant!" Then gazing at me, "The thing is, I like your company. You make me laugh. You don't have to answer this, but how do I make *you* feel?"

"Younger."

"Well there you are. My feminine charms have worked their magic."

I sighed, "All a bit late now, Helena. It's been a quite few years since I woke up with a lady beside me."

We were approaching the pub when she said, "Quite honestly, you look nothing like your age, did you never think of joining a dating site?"

"What and take some frail old dear out to a Tea Dance? What if I gave her a passionate snog and kissed a tooth right out?"

We entered the pub with Helena holding on to me, convulsed with laughter.

"What would I do then, swallow it or meekly hand it back?"

"Stop it," she gasped, her laughter that infectious, all in the pub were grinning.

I had a steak sandwich the pub was famed for, but Helena had nothing more than the game soup.

On the return journey, I admitted there had been romantic liaisons before the lean spell, but all the women had thought it their right, to take over the house as if a man living alone couldn't manage.

"I wouldn't do that," Helena replied.

That sent a jolt straight through me, but I shelved the little topic for another time. Instead, I said, "Starting a relationship didn't seem that hard. Finishing it was the difficult thing. When you think about it, it's an absolute cheek. I wouldn't dream of going into a woman's place and immediately start criticising it, cleaning it and rearranging the furniture. One actually started humming as she busied herself."

Helena looked at me and feigning mystification, said, "My word, you have been a bit of a dark one. So how many poor discarded ladies are we talking about here?"

"Look Helena, I love female company, but not to the point of becoming completely ensnared. They seem to like what they see and then do all they can to alter it. I suppose it's that instinct you were talking about.

Never leaves them. Also, you'd think a bit of fun and male company would suffice, but no, they demand to know, 'Where's all this leading?' Insisting on commitment as if they could still get pregnant."

By the time we arrived back, the night had that cold, pitch black feel that induces a shudder. I offered to drive Helena to her car, but then suggested, wouldn't it make more sense if she stayed the night, for I was quite willing to make do with the sofa.

To my surprise, Helena accepted, but insisted, she should be the one to sleep on the sofa. I made the thing as comfortable as possible and said, "It would be lovely if you shared my bed, but I'm told I've become a bit of a snorer."

Helena laughed.

"Don't like to admit it, but when sometimes, I even wake myself up, there's no denying it. When this unfortunate development first started, I'd sit bolt upright to demand, 'Who made that noise? Is there someone in the room?'"

Helena's eyes sparkled when she laughed.

I continued, "But no. Have to admit it, I've turned into a bit of an old snorer. There are variations mind you. There's the rhythmic snore, diddly-dum, as if I'm on a train and sometimes my nose gets a bit blocked, which makes a whine like a mosquito."

"You're joking!"

"No I'm not. Honestly! I woke the one morning smacking myself round the ear."

My last sight of Helena, was her sitting on the sofa, convulsed with laughter

Part Two

Part Two

Chapter Nine

To my huge disappointment, when I descended next morning, I found Helena had gone. The sheets and blankets had been left neatly folded and she'd even gathered up yesterday's newspaper, two magazines and numerous pieces of notepaper I'd scrawled on, to leave them stacked neatly on the coffee table, but there was no note explaining why she'd left.

I looked in the kitchen, almost expecting to see the washing up done, but no, the few items were still waiting by the sink.

Just then, a phone rang in the sitting room, not like the ring I'd heard that day when out walking, but more of a bleep, bleep. It was coming from over by the sofa and so I lifted the pile of blankets, but there was no sign. I found nothing behind the cushions, but when I pulled one of the main seating cushions forward, there it was, pulsating. It was the same device I'd found in the woods, but she'd obviously altered the ringtone.

"Helena?"

"Oh you've found it. Where was it?

"It had slipped down the back of a cushion. Would you like me to bring it to you?"

"You are an angel, but no, hang on to it for a while. It's my spare. I still have the one that matters. You won't be able to get into it without my help, but I'll show you what all the various bits and options are for, when we next meet."

"A bit wasted on me, Helena. A clever eight-year-old might appreciate it, mind you."

She laughed, then asked, "Did you find your keys?"

"No, I haven't looked."

"I let myself out and posted them back through the letter box."

"Where are you?"

"Haven't time to explain at the moment. All I can say is, I was called away. I'm afraid I'll be gone some time."

"I thought you said, you'd retired."

"We never completely retire, but as the world moves on, we're needed less and less. The bright new things forge their own contacts and what us have-beens still know, gradually becomes irrelevant."

"Have you a charger for this phone?"

"It doesn't need one. Don't ask me how, but during the day, it somehow charges itself."

"So can my phone contact this, or the one you have?"

"Don't even try, it won't work. It's best I contact you via that spare one. Thank you for everything, but I really have to fly. Big hug, byee."

I must admit, the call left me feeling a bit down in the dumps. The thought of walking to the stream or having a coffee in the Royal, just didn't seem like fun anymore. Shouldn't admit this, but there was a hint of perfume on her pillow and giving it a wishful hug, I savoured the aroma. Then chided myself, 'Silly old devil. At your age!'

I put the bedding away and made myself some breakfast. Toast marmalade and mug of tea. I didn't feel in the mood to bother with cooking anything like eggs or bacon. Now she was no longer there, came the realisation, Helena had got into my system more than I'd realised. It was alright for her, brought alive by some new mission, too busy to bother herself with the dull surroundings she'd left behind. Yes, it's always the one left behind who suffers the most.

Out of interest, I know she had told me it wouldn't work, but thinking, 'It won't hurt to try,' I decided to ring her number using my phone, but received a depressing, 'This call cannot be placed,' sort of message. Then I checked her phone, daring to press the only button, a green one, but nothing happened. I swiped the screen a couple of times, but the thing lay sleek, black and dormant.

I wasn't in the mood for doing anything in particular, but decided to shake myself out of my torpor, shave, shower and then go for a walk. Without any idea in mind regarding where to walk exactly, I found myself on the edge of the woodland, where I'd first heard the mysterious ringing that had led to this adventure. Meeting Helena had happened as if I'd been blessed by some magic charm, but it was no use trying to recreate it, for that magic was now gone and the woodland was as drab as my mood. What had been vibrant growth was now either brittle black remnants, or whitened dead reminders of that glorious autumn day. The grass was still green, but even that had a sullenness, moping in wet dense clumps that soaked my shoes. Should have worn wellies.

I ascended the banking to my right, managing not to slip on the mud and walked to where I'd first found Helena's phone. I was amazed to see that the strange circular flattened area I'd noticed that day was still there and just stood staring, wondering what had caused it. With summer's growth now brittle and the ferns having that rusty look, the impression appeared even more pronounced. Touring the clearing's perimeter, I expecting to see some sort of track left by a tractor, but found nothing. Quite strange.

I continued my walk as far as the bridge, but now the sight of the old mossed relic, *our* bridge, brought a feeling of sadness and I certainly didn't venture far side, to skid and slip on the path back to town.

First thing I did, when back home, was examine Helena's phone again. This time, on swiping the screen a message came up, 'Missed call.' It hadn't occurred to me to take the thing with me, but decided, from then on, I'd always carry it. After swiping it again and pressing the green button, in a vain attempt to return the call, I gave up, slipped it into a pocket and drove to the shops for some food.

I couldn't believe it. Some of the customers were still wearing covid masks. That's not a technically correct term, but you know what I mean. I felt like asking, 'D'you know how many coronavirus particles can fit on a pinhead?'

I'd probably get a terrified look, followed by, 'Leave me alone. I'm only doing my bit.'

'100 million! How do you think a grubby old mask will stop things that miniscule from getting through. If masks truly prevented their inhalation, you'd be dead. Suffocated!'

But I didn't say it. Why waste my time, for I'd probably only get sworn at and accused of being a conspiracy theorist. The sad thing was, some very good people did do their bit when the vaccines were first heralded as the silver bullet, but I won't go on about that now. I will quickly add, mind you, when people were truly scared, even though I knew the masks were virtually useless, I had no qualms about wearing one in a shop or crowded place. I did it more out of respect for others, rather than any good it might have done.

Then I remembered something, I was certain Helena would have found mirthful, for even when the pandemic was virtually over and the all clear had been sounded, I had still seen people walking along empty country roads, in the middle of nowhere, with a mask on. I'd even seen the 'odd one' driving alone, virtue signalling, proudly masked up.

'Oh Helena,' I thought. 'I chance upon a kindred spirit and now you're gone.' But once again, I chided myself.

I really had to get her out of my mind, but couldn't help another quick glance at her phone to check whether a message had been left.

It was early evening when I heard it ring. I pressed the green button and gritted my teeth, annoyed with myself, for I realised I must have sounded slightly breathless.

Following the first brief exchanges, I foolishly asked, "Where are you, Helena?"

"You know I can't tell you that."

"Of course. Stupid of me, but at least I can enquire as to your welfare. How are you?"

"Fine, but please pay attention, I don't have much time. You need to know how to work that device and I want you to listen carefully."

I did listen carefully and following instructions, managed to render it operational; for as long as it accepted the fingerprint of my right forefinger, when pressed against the small indent on the back, it would allow access. All considered quite basic technology these days of course, but like most fancy developments, it wasn't guaranteed to work, a bit like screen swiping, thus the need for the green button. Helena explained, that when in a tight spot, or out on field operations, instant contact was absolutely imperative. It would be pointless staring down at something supposedly that smart, it stubbornly refused to work.

"The green button is only for taking a call. It won't let you into the phone, except when I ring you and never--- never share that device with anyone."

"I wouldn't dream of it, Helena."

"No, I know you wouldn't. Sorry, it's my training. Cover all options, all possibilities and never assume."

"Well, it doesn't seem to stop you assuming what's in my mind."

"I told you, I'm not a mind reader, but analysing possibilities usually leads to a limited number of probabilities and from those a judgement can be posited."

"You make it sound very mechanical."

"I'm sorry, it's all that training I had, plus there were the rigorous six-monthly updates."

Following a long pause, she said, "Sorry to sound a bit like a schoolteacher, but I must stress, never try to access that thing, it's a sealed unit, sensitive to tampering. It will only work if I ring you and for God's sake don't lose it. There would be hell to pay if they found out I'd lent it to a--------"

Her voice trailing off, obviously left me wondering, 'To a what?' Other than being female, what was she that I wasn't? Plus what did she mean by, 'lent it?' Surely it had slipped down the back of the sofa. Or had it?

I was so bowled over to be talking to her again, however, I kept such suspicions to myself and instead, told her I'd been for a walk down by the stream, to which she replied laughing, "Oh, you went to *our* bridge. We did have some lovely times." With that she was gone.

'Did have,' sounded a bit ominous and sitting there feeling slightly confused, there came to mind other interesting snippets I wished I'd mentioned, but as is often the case, it was too late.

There again, were they actually that interesting? The way she had so briefly breezed back into my life, run rings around me and then ended the call without even a proper farewell, left me feeling rather dull and old, to say the least.

Being such cutting-edge technology, even the machine I held in my hand seemed to mock me, for I couldn't even use it. What secrets did it hold? I would not be long in finding out.

Chapter Ten

It was not that evening, but the one following that Helena rang again. I actually felt quite buoyant as I answered. Having gone about the dull daily tasks, knowing it wouldn't be long before chatting to her again, I had felt my spirits rising, glowing with the fact, that although having considered myself past it, I'd had the pure luck of chancing on someone so wonderful. It had begun to make me feel rather special, for even when encountering those who spend a lifetime mooching and moaning, I could laugh it off, knowing I would soon be in what had become my little sanctuary, talking to a very special lady. Just thinking about it, lifted me from the winter gloom and high above those resenting anyone not sharing their misery. "What's he got to look so flaming happy about?"

When the call eventually came, Helena sounded genuinely pleased to be back in contact and explained, that having had a bit of spare time, she'd been researching what could be achieved, using the phone she'd mislaid.

So she was now using the word mislaid rather than lent. Was she covering a verbal slip or compounding it? I hadn't the heart to say anything, mind you, for with her being so excited and bubbly, why pierce something that had given my spirits such a lift? Men can be complete suckers when it comes to the little girl act.

Completely hooked, I listened to the almost breathless explanation. "It's quite incredible really. You're not going to believe it. Can't wait to see your reaction. Working it out was quite tricky, but I've taken notes and with luck it should work."

She asked me to activate my phone's interior as done before, then place it on the dining table, with the business end pointing at a blank section of wall. I did so and then could hear whirring as it took her phone's instructions. The final outcome almost made me jump with shock, for with the room being perfectly dark, Helena suddenly appeared as if actually there with me.

"That's incredible, Helena."

"I know, isn't it fun?"

"You seem different, almost glowing."

"The effect of seeing you, dear."

"I would like to think so, but you do, you seem different."

"Actually it's probably the effect of being transmitted. That sounds dramatic, doesn't it, but anyway what have you been up to?"

I just rattled off the few things I'd done and then told her I'd revisited the park and there was now a notice saying, it was an offence to feed the ducks. Such a thing of pleasure for children, could now incur a fine.

"Oh, one other bit of news; people are up in arms. You remember that man who came to the aid of the lady on the bus? Well, he's been charged with actual bodily harm."

"Poor man. He should have been given a medal. And what about, what's her name?"

"Karen? I don't know and there doesn't seem to be any news regarding the bloke in the frock either."

We chatted for a while longer and then when I vainly reached out to see if I could actually touch her, I must have looked quite comical, for her laughter was that instant and gleeful, it gave hint of what she must have been like as a teenager.

"It would be nice if you *could* touch me," was said with a coquettish smile.

I didn't comment, for I remembered, how as a youth walking to school, girls in the safety of a passing bus, would sometimes wave in that saucy manner one dreams of and yet become a personification of demureness, when meeting them later in the street.

I was told what amazing things were held within the phone and once she was back to help me, what explorations could be undertaken, which I must admit, sounded like a cornucopia, but it was a bit unnerving knowing my inability to get the hang of it, was likely to highlight even further our age difference. My own phone had a few basics, but even most of those I left unused, being quite happy to simply use the thing for communicating. When the light beam was finally sucked back into her device and Helena was gone, I know it sounds stupid, but I swear a trace of her perfume lingered.

When weather permitted, I still went for brisk walks around the usual circuits, exchanging greetings with dog walkers and when meeting the odd few regulars I recognised, I'd stop and chat awhile. Not so long back, there had been a school of regulars in the local pub I visited. All sorts; retired teachers, an ex-bank manager, a cheery delivery driver who popped in for lunch, a retired GP, a lady who had once worked on the supermarket checkout------like I said, all sorts. Now the pub was boarded up. With the car park, weed strewn, its walls disfigured by scrawled graffiti and the once welcoming porch littered with junk mail, it was a depressing sight. I had popped into other pubs, but most had become more interested in selling food than beer and if you stood at the counter like in the old days, you felt very much in the way and there was no conviviality, when sitting alone at a table.

It was no good moping about the lost past, however and I decided to do something positive. I would decorate the living room. It would not only cheer me up, it would look bright and fresh, for when Helena returned. The question like a devil within, of course plagued, 'Ah, but will she return?' There again, I had to stay positive.

Like most jobs of its type, the redecorating was 80% preparation. It's amazing how many gaps, cracks, flaky bits and small holes you don't notice until starting work. Even just washing and painting the ceiling made a vast difference, especially as temporarily, there were no curtains to impede the light.

I got the odd wave from passers-by, obviously cheered by someone having a go.

When deciding on the most suitable colour for the ceiling I'd been rather torn between, 'Invisible Seagull' and 'Elephant's Breath'---. No, of course I jest. A sensible off-white did the trick and a friend who'd been in the paint and decorating trade, advised me not to use the emulsion all trendy middle-class women seem to go for; 'Fiddle and Bollocks,' he called it. 'They wouldn't choose it if they had to use it,' he'd said before adding, 'There's no doubting the colours are good, but you can always use their colour code and get it mixed in a paint that doesn't grin at you, after the second coat.' He said, that on one job, he'd had to apply five coats and then still had go round dabbing at unevenness grinning through.

The walls took two coats as normal, then I spent a further half hour, firming up the odd wispy patch. I won't go into all the details of sanding, filling, undercoating and all that masking tape business, when doing the woodwork, only to say I was very particular when cutting in around the edges.

It took six days hard work in all, just for a visitor to glance and say, "Oh that looks nice." They'd have soon noticed if it hadn't been done properly, mind you. As I sat there with curtains and furniture back in place,

I thought, 'All that crawling about and you can't even see half the skirting boards.'

During those six days, Helena phoned twice and I entertained her in the bedroom. Obviously, the room was blackened, but even so, she had realised I wasn't in the parlour. What a lovely old word.

On the first call, she said she had set up her own phone so that it would hear any questions I might like to ask and provide the answers on its screen. She said she'd made it into a game, for it would appear, she was the fount of all knowledge, rather than her cutting-edge phone, connected to the latest lightning-fast wizardry, flashing the answers.

Of course Helena had wanted to know what I'd been doing, but there wasn't much to tell her, as I'd been immersed in the redecorating job, but kept that a secret. I wanted the new look to surprise her when she next visited.

Eventually she said, "Go on then, ask me something? Anything you like."

"Who won the FA cup in 1952?"

She groaned, "Not those sort of questions! Something difficult. Newcastle United beat Arsenal 1-0, if you must know."

"How far is it to the moon?"

"Miles or kilometres?"

"Miles of course."

"On average, 238,855."

"How many Amazonian tribes are there?"

Helena answered instantly, "Between 400 to 500. Nobody's really sure."

"When did cannibalism die out in the Fijian Islands?"

Again came an immediate answer, "1867. The missionary, Reverend Thomas Baker was the last known victim. Whose to say though, old customs die hard and their strange culinary practices could have continued unrecorded. What a strange question, by the way."

"I've got a good one. How many different ways are there, to deal a deck of cards."

"Ah, a question close to my heart. Probably more ways than there are stars in the firmament."

"Really? I've been told the combinations are beyond belief, but I hadn't imagined that many."

"It's like a glorious infinity. What a clever question."

Helena looked quite dreamy, as if basking in the heavens and yet this was the lady who on that evening at the mossed bridge had professed to have a limited understanding of them.

The game went on for a while longer, but then, with a cheeky kiss blown, Helena, my star lady was gone. I sat staring at the wall, for with having nothing more than the further grind of redecorating to look forward to, I felt completely leaden.

When Helena next called, my spirits were on the up again, as I'd reached the point in the job where you know you've cracked it. My decorator friend had said, he loved the smell of gloss paint and on seeing my puzzled look, went on to explain, it meant he'd soon be getting paid.

I won't bother you with the details of the ensuing question-answer game, other than say Helena's replies were that instant, it was hard to imagine she was actually reading them. I informed her of the change of venue, for when she next called.

"We'll be back in the parlour."

"Oh goody," she said, clapping her hands and putting on her little girl act again. "Shall we play parlour games?"

"What sort of parlour games?"

"Well, I could appear as your fantasy girl. Perhaps dressed as a nurse, French maid, police woman, or----I know,--- I could dress as a schoolgirl."

"No Helena. That would be demeaning. You are my fantasy girl already. Please come just as you are."

"I was only teasing," she said laughing. "Where on earth would I find a French maid's outfit, stuck out here."

When once more alone in the darkness, I wondered, "Stuck out where?"

Wherever she was, she'd had a profound effect on me, for I no longer seemed to get those anxiety dreams, where having left a lively, congenial setting to nip out to a nearby shop, I'd not be able to find my way back again and end up miles away, completely lost.

Also, she'd caused me to take a good look at myself and my small abode. Following the success of the living room enterprise, I tidied up the patch of ground in front of the house. I raked and rooted out leaves, prised up the weeds and visited a reclamation yard for something to give a definite edge to the path and small circular rose garden. They had quite a stock based on Victorian designs and it's amazing the difference the rope-topped edging made.

Then turning attention to myself, I visited the barbers, followed by a drive to a nearby town that still had a traditional men's outfitters. Looking in the full-length mirror at a man wearing a crisp looking jacket of light checked fabric above dark slacks, I had to agree with the proprietor, that the combination had seemed to have taken years off me. Now feeling thoroughly in the mood, I also bought a dark blue V-necked sweater, plus two shirts and was almost loath to take my old clothes home with me.

The notion of visiting a shoe shop for a new pair of brogues, also crossed my mind, but I decided to have my old pair given a thorough service, so to speak. Not only did they need soling and heeling, a bit of stitching was required where creases had opened into small cracks. It would be good to have my old friends back, but I said, "Nothing too slippery please," meaning the soles. For after all, it was winter and at my age, I didn't want to draw unwanted attention, by gliding down an icy incline like an errant curling stone.

Next came the sofa-bed idea. As said, Helena and I, although given to slightly flirtatious banter at times, had basically no more than a platonic relationship and so if she did decide to stay the night in future, I needed another bed. She couldn't be expected to make do with my old sofa.

Trawling through the internet I chanced on a deal, that tempting, I immediately phoned the firm. The man was incredibly helpful and explained they were moving into completely new lines and outing old stock. Payment included delivery.

I was contacted the day before its arrival and I made sure my car was parked outside, rather badly in fact, for the space when vacated, would be sufficient for a van to park. They arrived when they said they would and I moved my vehicle to a friend's front drive. He'd converted his patch of garden into a soulless looking parking area.

The two men struggled with the massive cardboard box into the hallway. One said, "Mind the light," before, without another word, they slipped the weighty burden into a vertical position, where it stood much higher than the entrance to the front room. It was swivelled, pulled from the base and with the one man easing it into a horizontal position, the other, ensured the far end didn't scrape the hallway wall. Then together, they carried it in like a massive coffin and I was asked where I wanted it putting. They insisted on unwrapping the sofa for my inspection and then offered to take all the plastic and cardboard wrapping away. On my proffering of a five-pound note as a tip, one said, "No, that's alright, thanks mate," and off they went leaving me feeling stunned. If only all business deals could be such a pleasure. I couldn't speak more highly of them. It really lifted the spirits, as do the ladies in the grocers and dry cleaners, who address me as, 'Darling.' It's meant as no more than a friendly gesture, but makes it such a pleasure to enter their premises.

Then I remembered reading somewhere, a number of firms were forbidding such familiarity; something to do with sexism. What was the world coming to? It seems, a certain group of fanatics won't be satisfied until we all become androgenous zombies referring to each other as 'They,' or 'Person.'

A friend who owned an estate car helped me get rid of the old sofa at the local tip. I'd of course checked for coins that might have slipped into its innards and asked the council official, which skip to put it in? "Or would it benefit someone, if I left it amongst the items for sale?" He took one look and said, "General rubbish."

As you can imagine, I was in quite a chipper mood when Helena next contacted me. She appeared as if actually there in the parlour, but wearing nothing more than a blouse, hardly long enough to give a semblance of decency.

As she hoisted herself up onto a stool, I said, "Helena! You're not wearing any----"

Stretching out a leg she said rather grandly, "I know, but I thought boots would look rather ridiculous without leggings or jeans." Then leaning forward she added, "And don't be so prudish, no-one can see me."

"Well I can."

"But you don't mind, do you?"

Of course I didn't mind, but the whole experience knocked me completely out of my stride. In fact, sitting there transfixed, I found it a struggle to continue a genial conversation. I'd often imagined such a thing happening, what red-blooded male hasn't? No don't answer that; but the strange thing is, my reaction was totally the opposite to what you'd expect and when she finally slipped away, blowing a kiss, I couldn't work out why; but following that initial pulse-thumping shock, I had begun to feel rather saddened.

I sat for quite some time trying to figure it out. In the end, it suddenly dawned on me, Helena seemed to be trying too hard. In an attempt to gauge what I might have actually wanted from a woman, I'd not yet even kissed, she'd got it wrong. More than that, it was almost as if the little cameo had not been her idea. Plus, when you think about it, it was me that should have felt vulnerable. I was the old fogey, whereby, she in comparison was a bright young thing. The experience brought a sadness that was quite unsettling. Who exactly was she?

Part Three

Part Three

Chapter Eleven

Nowhere near as unsettling as what happened next, mind you. It was about a week later and returning to the house about midday, I detected the faint aroma of perfume in the hallway, then on opening the front room door, was stunned by the sight of Helena sitting on the new sofa.

"Well, you *have* been busy," was said, almost as if in judgement.

"Helena, what a wonderful surprise, but how did you get in?"

She was wearing the weather-proof coat of that strange dark material, her usually pretty tresses hung lank and her eyes looked frighteningly hollow. Had she somehow managed to melt in here on a phone-beam, leaving the essence of Helena I'd known stuck far side of the door? Although obviously glad to see her, it had a macabre feel that was truly unsettling.

Looking almost too tired to speak, she said, "You need to get the front door lock replaced. That thing wouldn't stop a child."

"How long have you been sitting here? Can I get you anything? You look worn out."

"I'll be fine."

She actually had the deflated look of a woman, who having had a bit of a fling and things not going entirely to plan, had been left with no alternative, other than returning to her safe, but boring old spouse.

"Can I get you something to eat, Helena? Or a cup of tea?"

"No. Please don't fuss."

"It's so good to have you here again. Actually here in person."

This brought a distant smile. "It was tough," she said, looking truly weary. "Ease of return depends on so many factors, but believe me this was a tough one."

Of course, there was no point me asking for details and so I just said, "Well at least you're safe now."

"Thank you. You do make me feel safe. You've no idea how grateful I am, but now I need to ask a very big favour."

I noticed a glint of life had returned to her eyes, obviously hoping to enhance the plea, but the effort of summoning it, seemed to drain the life from her limbs.

With my hands gently holding her shoulders, I said, "No please, don't get up. It won't be a problem, just ask."

"I need a place to stay."

Trying not to look too elated, I said, "You can stay here. Stay as long as you like. In fact that sofa you're sitting on, opens up as a bed."

"You're so kind. I've been sitting here worrying myself silly."

"You've no need to worry, Helena?" Feeling buoyed and reeling slightly from my sudden change of fortune, I said, "Now look! I must get you something to eat. It won't take a minute and it will make you feel much better."

"Thank you, but no. If you don't mind, I just need somewhere to lie down."

"Yes of course." Thinking for a moment, I said, "It would be easier if you had my bed. I'll change the sheets. What happened to your own place, by the way?"

"I gave that up when I left. All my things are in storage. Oh, before I do anything else, I need to recharge the phones. If you bring me the one I lost, I'll plug it in down here. Hadn't envisaged using it to the extent we did. Poor thing must be about to give up the ghost."

She hauled up the large satchel, I'd seen leaning against the sofa and laying it on her lap, undid the straps of the upper section. Inside were numerous flaps, pockets and integral boxes and withdrawing a small metal pin, she squinted as if about to thread a needle. Carefully probing a certain spot on the base of the phone, caused a tiny aperture to flick open, into which she inserted the end of a lead. A two pinned plug was withdrawn from a pocket in the satchel, to complete the assembly and she asked, "OK to use that plug?"

I said, "Of course, but it won't work. That's a three-pin socket."

Producing the thinnest of plastic needles, she knelt down beside the plug and on standing said, "There that should do it."

It reminded me of Christmases years ago, when toys and gadgets were sold without plugs or batteries. With all the shops being shut for the holiday and impatient to use the gift, we'd poke the bare wire ends into a socket and jam them in with a nearby lamp plug. I realised, Helena, had obviously pressed the needle into topmost slot of the socket, for the pair below to open and allow insertion of the two-pin plug.

"With a bit of fiddling, that thing will fit most sockets," she explained. "Whether here or Outer Mongolia."

I carried her satchel upstairs. It was quite a weight. Obviously a special issue for operatives. I changed the bed linen, laid a clean towel ready and descended to inform my guest all was ready.

"You're so kind. I can't thank you enough."

"Now, what about that snack or at least a cup of tea?"

Helena sighed and said with a weak smile, "Oh, very well, but just a cup of tea. That will be fine, thank you."

"I'll bring it up shortly."

"Just a dash of milk and no sugar."

"Exactly how I like it," I called as she ascended the stairs.

I waited awhile. I could hear Helena was still in the bathroom and there would be no point in leaving the tea to go cold beside the bed. On hearing footsteps heading towards the bedroom, I switched the kettle on. I reckoned, by the time it had boiled and the tea had steeped awhile, sufficient time would have elapsed to allow her to don whatever and slip into bed.

I climbed the stairs and tapped on the door. "Helena?" I whispered.

Hearing no reply, I eased the door open and saw she was flat-out, as if lying in state, crowned by a towel wrapped around her head, like a huge white turban. A thin black wire trailed from the bedside socket, to up under the covers. She was obviously charging her own phone, but why it should be in bed with her remained a mystery.

Back downstairs, I sipped on her tea, deep in thought, trying to make sense of it all. I sat for such a time, I began to feel chilled and so turned up the thermostat for the heating to bring a bit of cheer. I only ever turn the bedroom radiator on if I happen to have been away during winter, for the north facing room can get so miserably cold, it almost feels damp, but with the heat now filtering upstairs, I imagined Helena to be feeling quite cosy.

Knowing a woman's eye would soon be cast over the kitchen, I gave everything a thorough clean; sink, worktops, cooker-top, window, floor. The job took well into the afternoon, leaving no time for a rest, as I needed to get on with the meal I had planned. A beef casserole. After searing the meat amongst browning onions, garlic and cheap red wine, I added it to the chopped vegetables, bought fresh from the market. I'd obviously seasoned the browning beef and then along with a chopped chili and mixed herbs, gave it the Lea and Perrins, jabbing the bottle to add five spurts of that mysterious relish, before committing all to the oven. The latter was one of the things I hadn't cleaned, but it wasn't particularly greasy and anyway, it wouldn't have looked particularly romantic, had I been caught mid-job.

I went to the foot of the stairs, but heard no sound of movement above.

Back in the kitchen, I peeled enough potatoes for two and left them immersed in a pot, ready for boiling.

Returning to the front room, I could see the streetlamps had come on and so drew the curtains. There was not much of interest on TV. I never watch 'soaps' and hate the reality shows. I'd seen snatches of them when visiting friends. In fact in the one house, it had given me such a headache trying to talk over it, I'd asked if they could possibly turn the set off. A number of couples I know, switch the TV on first thing in the morning and have it as a background noise, throughout the day and into the night, not even switching it off at mealtimes or when visitors arrive.

With still no sign of Helena, I remained sitting on the new front room facility, alone with my thoughts.

I remembered that when growing up, we didn't have much in the way of money or latest household gimmickry, but it was considered thoroughly rude to leave the TV on if visitors suddenly descended. On one winter's afternoon, with all ensconced in the dark confines of the TV room watching an absolute classic, something like, Legend of the Glass Mountain, an aunt and uncle happened to turn up unexpectedly.

"It's only us," they announced and probably wondered why we looked less than thrilled.

Regarding those that leave the TV on all day, I came to the conclusion it must be a comfort thing, or in some cases, used as a prop where the couple realised, they had absolutely nothing in common anymore.

Anyway, enough of reminiscing and postulating, for upstairs a wonderful woman lay in repose and I couldn't wait to converse with her again. There was still no sign of movement, however, and as I sat there dreaming up explorations I could take her on, I couldn't help it, but my tongue kept wandering to a small crater, top-left in the upper gum. It was a silly thing to keep doing, because where the aged dental work had lost its grip, it had left a jagged perimeter. I couldn't help it, mind you and thought, 'That will teach you, for joking about kissing old lady's gnashers out!'

Luckily, I'd managed to book myself into the dentist for the coming Thursday. I'd used him for years, but he was due for retirement; then what would I do? Dentists were becoming as rare as hen's teeth.

Sighing, I wondered what to do next and with still no sign of Helena, I picked up a book I'd started; persevering, partly out of determination, but largely on account of it being highly praised, to the point of it having been made into a film, but I not only found parts of the plot implausible, also some of the character's motives. I must have sounded like a right old geezer, when muttering things like, "Come off it! They wouldn't have done that. Not really." Regarding one section, I was amazed the editor hadn't intervened, asking, "Can you really expect readers to believe that this gang of artisans, just happen to turn up out of the blue and hack massive gate hinges from out of a castle wall without the guards above hearing a single thing?"

By now, as you can imagine, I was feeling rather peckish, made worse by a delicious aroma drifting into the room and on walking through to the kitchen, happened to glance at the wall mirror and remembering recent thoughts, muttered to myself, 'Don't make a fool of yourself, old fella. This could still all end in tears.'

With Helena having given no hint of gathering herself for an arising, I had turned the oven down to low, so the casserole hadn't dried out and as I now felt thoroughly ravenous, I didn't bother boiling the potatoes, but ate a bowlful straight from the pot, along with bread, fresh from a bakery to mop up the juice. I'd even buttered the bread and I tell you what, it was that tasty as it all melled together, I took another scoopful.

Finally, with Helena obviously still out for the count, I decided to leave her be and that explains why I happened to be the first person to use that brand-new sofa bed.

Next morning, I at last heard movement and Helena descended wearing one of my old linen shirts, a thing I'd chanced upon in a charity shop. It was collarless with a light grey mattress ticking design. She smiled and flopped against me, saying, "What a sleep! I needed that."

"I can see it's done you the world of good." She actually looked restored to her former glorious self and eying her standing there, barefoot and hair restrained by one of those bands that produce such a topknot look of wild abandonment, I said, "Well Helena, I have to say; that's the best I've ever seen that shirt look."

Her smile although gracious, held a hint of tolerance and she said, "You must think I'm awful, stealing your bed."

"No, not at all. In fact that sofa bed is surprisingly comfy."

I'd already had breakfast, two boiled eggs and toast and asked Helena what she would like?

Her reply of not needing anything, I found incredible and so persisted, listing the choices.

"Do I look as if I'm wasting away?"

I must admit, compared to the woman who had looked so drained the previous day, I had never seen such a transformation. In the end, probably just to please me, she settled on at least having a bowl of cornflakes and asked where the packet was.

"In the cupboard, top left of the cooker hood."

Then seeing her about to reach up, I said, "No Helena. I think it might be best if I get it for you," which elicited a provocative giggle.

How easily a pretty woman can make grown men melt at the knees.

On my enquiring, whether it would be alright if I were to get some clothes from the bedroom, she answered, "Of course. Why are you asking? It's your bedroom." Then, when just about to sprinkle the cornflakes, she said with eyes sparkling, "Oh, I hope you don't mind. Don't be cross, but I've hung a few of my things out to air."

I ascended the stairs, pushed open the bedroom door and stood looking in sheer amazement. If there had recently been a clothes-flinging fiesta, it couldn't have made more of an impact. Diaphanous garments hung from everywhere; wardrobe door, curtain rail, bedside lamp, the small easy chair, the two pictures and even the central light fitting. Her satchel lay fully open on the bed, containing plastic purses and pouches and amongst all lay brassieres and thin lacy filaments which

I presumed, would serve as knickers once pulled up and snapped into place. Gazing around I wondered, how had so much come from inside such a small piece of luggage? I was in my own bedroom, my own safe cave, and yet was now standing amid a world, I'd always known I'd never come close to understanding.

Without disturbing the adorning drapery, I managed to ease out sufficient dull garb for the day and retired to the bathroom to wash and dress. Here again were signs of a recent incursion. A make-up pouch lay open with the tiny plastic tubes, jars and brushes on display and my shaving mirror stood propped up atop the laundry basket. I removed the chair from the small impromptu beauty salon and returned it to its place against the wall.

Roughly seven minutes later I was back down in the kitchen. Thanking Helena for swilling the few breakfast things, I peered out into the back yard. It didn't look like a bad day and so suggested we might venture out somewhere.

Any idea of a country ramble was out of the question, for the only substantial clothes she had, were those she'd arrived in and with her telling me she felt as if still recuperating from a long illness, I suggested doing something simple, like popping into town for a coffee at the Royal.

With her already having put her face on, it didn't take long to ready herself and risking the bus once again, we were able to sit together on a trip without incident.

Being a week day, there weren't many in the coffee lounge and we again sat by the tall sash windows, bathed in light that angled shapes across the carpet.

We chatted about this and that; the front room redecoration; I mentioned my upcoming dental appointment; asked about retrieving her belongings from the storage unit; the whereabouts of her car, but what I really wanted to get to grips with, was how the hell had she had managed to harness a technology, that amazing, it had allowed her to appear as if right there in the room with me. Infuriatingly, I received just shrugs and hazy replies and regarding the car, all I got was, "Oh, that's gone." She really was an enigma.

The only thing of substance said on what I assumed to have been some sort of highly advanced hologram, was for me to promise never to mention our little secret to others. Well, I was hardly likely to betray this amazing woman, that so late in my life, had arrived like a gift from the gods.

Our peace was suddenly disturbed, for what looked like a group of recent retirees entered in a state of total indecision and as they fussed and pithered about, I noticed Helena eying them in that calculating manner cats have.

"What about over there?" one man asked.

"Or here," said one of the women.

"That looks quite nice over there," another said.

Helena muttered, "Just sit down for God's sake," and then groaned as they headed our way.

Then came the fuss over what to order. I expected the waitress to glance in our direction with an eye-roll of frustration, but no, she stood patiently waiting.

When one of the men stood up and apologised, saying nature called, the waitress politely dismissed herself, saying she would return when they were ready.

"What a nice girl," said one of the ladies. "So patient."

"Patience of a ruddy saint," Helena muttered.

"Shh," I said laughing. "I think she heard you."

Helena had yet again said exactly what I'd been thinking.

By the time the coffee and assortment of dainties finally arrived they had all settled into what might be described as, a far calmer roosting mode, but then began the vigorous sugar rattling ritual, before pouring sachet contents into coffee.

I pricked an ear, for the conversation had now turned to recent news regarding the covid virus.

"Do you remember all that nonsense about the hand sanitisers?" said one of the men.

"Yes, fat lot of good they did," came a reply.

"And the masks!"

"Bloody ridiculous," declared one woman. "Damn things could bring on a coughing fit. I swear they all thought I should have been in quarantine."

"Oh, I still keep mine," said another. "You never know."

"With a face like that, I shouldn't wonder," I muttered, causing Helena to almost choke on a sip of coffee.

One of the men asked, not caring that the whole room could hear, "And what about those ridiculous lockdowns?"

"Criminal," came a reply.

"Whoever dreamt up that crazy notion, ought to be locked up themselves."

"For life," came the trumping comment.

This I found amazing, for what had probably scared them all rigid, they were now talking about as if nothing other than something that evoked a little nostalgia and the measures they had probably once backed to the hilt, they were now proclaiming to have always known what hyped-up nonsense they had been. Also, what they were now discussing quite openly, would until very recently, have had the covid warriors and virtue signallers screeching, "Granny killers and conspiracy theorists!"

I leaned across and said to Helena, "How quickly things change."

"Not surprising really. People are like sheep."

"I know, but in all fairness, they actually sound like good people. After all that pressure from the media, scare mongering and folks petrified of being stigmatised by the dreaded anti-vaxxer accusations, it's good to hear such honesty."

"Mmm," was Helen's reply.

"It's alright for you. You were probably out on some foreign mission, but England became a country I no longer recognised. The people seemed cowed as if they'd had the stuffing knocked out of them and any notion of debate regarding, masks, lockdowns, or vaccines was tantamount to questioning a new religion. Cult members would simply sneer, 'anti-vaxxer,' or 'conspiracy theorist' and that would be that,--- end of discussion!"

Even though receiving no more than a patient look, I still persevered. "Even the media gave favour to such comments as, 'Strand the unvaccinated on some remote island,' or, 'Deny them access to the NHS!'"

"Were you ever vaccinated?" Helena asked.

I was about to say, 'I've had numerous vaccines over the years,' but she'd of course meant the covid vaccine. I replied, that luckily, I had not and went on to explain the circumstances.

The following is a short resume'. When the vaccines first became available, I'd been staying with friends abroad and like most, thought them to be a miracle of science, arriving just in time to save the world, but as I was in an area with virtually no infections, I decided to bide my time. In England, I'd have received the shot for free, whereas where I was residing, I'd have been charged a hefty price for something I might not need.

So, I kept a low profile and when the next vaccine requirement message appeared on my phone, dear old Blighty had reached that hyper-hysterical stage, meaning that if I did return to take up the offer, I'd have been forced like a pariah into quarantine for ten days, before even being allowed near a clinic.

My friends were tremendous and told me I was best sitting it out until things calmed down.

Covid did arrive locally, as we knew it would, but people were sensible and in actual fact, even though only half the population had received the vaccine, there were very few fatalities. One 92-year-old living in a nearby village, did die sadly, but his 80-year-old brother recovered and is still going strong. More disturbing were the accounts going around, concerning vaccine side effects. A healthy farmer in his fifties, living in a nearby village dropped dead two days after receiving the first jab and another became semi-paralysed and as far as I know, is still bedridden to this day. As you can imagine, nobody queued for further vaccines once those sort of stories got about. Teachers, librarians, doctors, nurses, police officers, post office employees and those in government service, had no choice, however, it was mandatory. Criminal when you think about it.

Then came similar heart-rending details of vaccine damage from the UK, Australia, the US and the major

European nations. Not via the media, I hasten to add. A number of highly respected doctors, risked everything, their careers and reputations, by daring to speak out and were duly pilloried. One MP raised the issue twice in Parliament, but incredibly, hardly anyone turned up to listen. The more I read of the medical details of what had in fact had been an experiment, a new technology rushed into operation without the usual five-year trial period, the more I realised I'd had a lucky escape and decided I would never risk taking any mRNA vaccine, no matter what it may have been prescribed for.

Turning to Helena, I said, "People still won't listen to reason, but there again, you can hardly blame them. Who wants to hear they might have a potential death shot or life changer working away inside them."

"Sounds like a perfect way to lose friends."

"Then, if you try the logic; the vaccines didn't stop covid infection or transmission, they come up with the same lame mantra, 'But they lessen the severity of the disease.'

We sat in silence for a while. The group next to us was shuffling about, obviously on the point of leaving.

"Don't forget your glasses, Ron," one woman said.

"Gosh, thanks, Marge. I'll be forgetting my head next."

"We must make sure we leave that nice girl a decent tip," another woman said. Then looking in our direction,

"You must think us an awful bunch of ditherers. Comes with age I'm afraid."

"Did you enjoy yourselves?" I asked.

"Yes, very much so."

"Excellent, that's the main thing." I not only meant it, I also regretted the comment made about her friend's face, but of course, once those words are out there you can't haul them back in.

"What a nice man," I heard her say to a colleague.

Turning to Helena, I said, "Bless her. She apologised for her age, but the daft thing is, I wouldn't mind betting I'm a fair bit older than she is."

"It's my influence, dear. I've awoken the boy in you."

There was no arguing with that, but I also recalled, 'There's no fool like an old fool.'

Then came the memory of another apt line. If Mandy Rice-Davies had been told,---- the authorities have now accepted the covid vaccines don't really work as first stated, but assure us they lessen the severity of the disease,---- she'd have said, "They would say that wouldn't they."

"Helena?"

"Mmm?"

"Don't suppose you'd know who Mandy Rice-Davies was. You're too young."

Following a flicker of face freeze, as witnessed before, she replied. "Profumo affair, 1963."

I was obviously quite impressed. I could actually have gone on more about the vaccines, for I found it staggering, that even though the worst of the pandemic was now over, the excess death rate in the developed world, was still running way above average and yet no-one seemed willing to investigate. It was the perfect block-buster news story and yet all the papers steered clear. I suppose, having helped coerce the population into taking the vaccines, to do their bit and save granny, they could hardly now suddenly admit, the cure could end up doing more harm than the disease. I just hoped and prayed, the vaccine-induced spike proteins working in the body, gradually dissipate, leaving survivors unharmed, for all my friends had had at least two doses and I didn't want my opinions finally vindicated, only to find I was the last of the Mohicans.

I suddenly realised, I'd not asked Helena about her vaccine status.

Without any hint of facial expression, she said, "Everything was arranged."

"I suppose, with all the travelling you did, it was mandatory. Two shots at least."

"We had the paperwork and so there was not a problem."

"A vaccine passport that proved you'd had two injections that didn't stop you catching the virus or passing it on? Those flaming things were not worth the paper they were printed on."

"Yes, they were strange times. I knew, it didn't make a scrap of sense, but I had the paperwork, everyone was satisfied and so we were able to go about our business without let or hindrance."

"But don't you realise, you've probably all put your lives at risk?"

"We were furnished with the right paperwork," she said with a sigh.

"Oh, sorry. I was a bit slow there. Now I see what you mean."

With a gentle finger wag, she added, "And, not a word."

Chapter Twelve

That evening, seeing Helena was starting to look tired again, I suggested it would be easier if we stuck to the previous night's sleeping arrangements and looking thoroughly grateful, she planted a kiss on the side of my face and retired early.

I wasted an hour trying to contact a person willing to upgrade the security on my front door, but apart from a man who said he could do it in the new year, no-one seemed interested in such a fiddling little job and so I decided to tackle it myself.

The next morning, with Helena still in her boudoir, (my bedroom) I left a note and drove to the industrial estate on the edge of town. I remembered there was a small shop that specialised in tools and handy household repair items and selected a lock and treated myself to a new chisel. I had a few in my tool box, but the 3/8th chisel was as blunt as a screwdriver. When I went to pay, I was completely taken aback, for the gaunt looking youth, with his, 'Oh so clever,' overweening look, asked for my address.

I said, "You're joking!"

"No sir, it's company policy."

I had intended to pay by card, but to avoid any further invasion of privacy I counted out the cash and slid it towards him.

"Sorry sir, we are not allowed to take cash."

"This is getting ridiculous," I said and on handing over my card, added, "And don't dare ask for my address again, because I'm not giving it. All I want, is to buy two piddling little bits and you make it seem as if I might have criminal intentions in mind, or could be money laundering."

Back at the house, Helena was now up and told me she had helped herself to breakfast. I related my tale of frustration and when storming into, "Everything's getting too damned clever and difficult these days! I bet the bony blighter wouldn't tell me where **he** lived!" she laughed and said, "You are funny. He probably just wanted to add you to the mailing list."

"They can forget that! I get enough junk mail as it is. They even want to know your name when you're buying a coffee. I was in a service station early one morning and got asked in that lispy way they have, 'Woth's your name?'

'Why?'

'Well quite litrallee,---- I have to wite it on the side of the mug.'

"I still don't see why."

"Well litrallee,---- it means I can call your name when the coffee's ready."

"Look, I don't know whether you've noticed, but apart from you, I'm quite literally the only other bugger in the place!'

Helena, obviously tickled, said, "You shouldn't let these little grievances get to you."

"But it's true, Helena. Even doing the simplest of things, these days, is either invasive or like pulling a flaming tooth!"

That reminded me, I had the dentist's appointment on the morrow and so decided to get the lock job sorted straight away.

I'm probably one of the most reluctant odd job men you could ever meet, with no natural flair whatsoever, but where needs must----. The job was finished by early afternoon and even though a skilled man would have probably done it in half the time, having put away the drill etc and tidied up, I felt quite pleased with myself and suggested a quick visit to the park. On the way, I ate the sandwich Helena had made and even though she avowed she'd helped herself to similar, for some reason I didn't quite believe it.

Later, with there being absolutely no suggestion of me having my room back, I spent yet another night, downstairs, feeling like a lodger in my own house.

The following morning, I nipped up to tell Helena I was off to the dentist and asked her to please help herself to breakfast. Sitting up in bed, diligently working on her laptop, she glanced up as if an office junior had entered and on my suggesting we collect her belongings later, all I got was a tolerant smile.

She did add, as I left the room, "Hope it doesn't hurt," and then, when halfway down the stairs I heard, "Haven't you forgotten something?"

On my return, I noticed her rather remote look had been replaced by a gleeful grin and pointing to her right cheek she said, "My kiss."

At the surgery, my friendly dentist explained why simply gluing the fallen denture back into place was not an option, then having cleared the site of debris for the drilling of ancient root canal workings to receive the pins, construction of a slender stump was meticulously undertaken. I made an appointment for its crowning, a week hence.

With driving there and back and having that preparatory job completed, two hours had elapsed. Hardly time for Helena to have undertaken anything major, but on returning home, I found her belongings had not only been delivered, they'd been unpacked and were now all upstairs in my bedroom.

Helena said, "It made such a clutter in the hallway, I thought it best if he helped me bring it all up here out of the way."

I could see clothing and footwear and of course the famed cashmere coat which hung in splendour, covering one of my pictures. A picture my mother had painted.

"I hope I haven't upset you," Helena said with that winsome, 'Please don't be cross,' expression some women can perfect.

"What about all your other things? Hope they're not imminent." I of course had in mind, pink furry slippers, giant cuddly toy, all the small cushions that need flinging off the bed before being able to pull the covers back and of course the box of curlers, hair dryer and hefty packing cases full of kitchen utensils.

"Oh, I got rid of all that other stuff a while back; I don't wear pink furry slippers and the curlers and hair dryer are under the bed."

"But how did you get it all here? You no longer have a car."

"We ladies have our ways."

'There's no doubting that,' I thought, as I descended to my lodger's pad.

Looking outside, I could see a parking space had just come available directly in front of the house and so nipped out to take advantage. On locking up, I noticed my neighbour approaching wearing a slightly puzzled expression that precedes a question. He had a certain native wit, but for some reason, I never quite trusted the man.

"Excuse me for asking, squire---"

That did it! Already my hackles were on the rise, for I hated that form of address and if he'd have asked about Helena, I'd have told him to mind his own business.

"Hope you don't think I'm being nosey, but who was that strange article that was here earlier."

"I imagine you are referring to the delivery driver."

"Weirdest delivery driver I ever clapped eyes on. All dressed in black and thin as a drainpipe."

"Probably a devotee of some new youth cult."

"Nothing youthful about that blighter. Hard to put an age to him in fact. And thin------!

"Oh look. Your cat's just gone inside my house. It's never done that before."

As I hastened up the path, I heard, "Seen more meat on a jockey's whip!"

There was no sign of the interloper in the hallway and the front room door was shut, meaning it must have gone upstairs. Tapping on the bedroom door, I pushed it further ajar and there was the cat looking perfectly at home on my bed.

"I've got a new friend," said Helena, stroking beneath its raised chin with a forefinger.

I allowed the cat to stay for a while and then popped it back into the neighbour's front garden.

That evening, I prepared a meal, only simple fare, fried onions, garlic, fish, peas, rice and a squeeze of lemon and when Helena again declined to eat anything, I told her it was totally baffling and asked; no in fact I demanded to know the reason why. I was worried she might have been suffering from some kind of bulimia, but she assured me she wasn't and explained, the solution to what was obviously a conundrum, lay in the special tablets she took.

She showed me some small white pills

I stared and said, "You can't possibly survive on those."

"Well sorry to gainsay you, but I'm living proof that I do."

I had to admit, having fully recovered from whatever journey had been involved when returning to my door, she now looked the picture of health. In fact, on our recent trip to the Royal, I'd noticed a number of ladies we'd passed, eying us both and giving an inner sigh, as if envying a couple in love. It was all quite flattering for me of course and I have to say when out together, whether with the regal cashmere Helena, or the fun-loving country girl, she did give the impression that emotionally, she belonged to me. Quite staggering really, for we'd not even exchanged a proper kiss.

Then I thought, would she really want to kiss an old fogey like me? The mere thought probably disgusted her and yet she played the part as if we truly were a couple. To what extent this could be tested, however, was a constant worry, for looming close, was a dinner engagement with friends. It had been described as supper, but whether supper or dinner it would still amount to the same thing and what would be their reaction, when Helena declined their 'spot of supper' and instead popped a couple of white pills?

I absolutely dreaded it. Would be better for all concerned if I rang and apologised, explaining Helena was in a dark room suffering from migraine, but that would only delay the inevitable, for they'd probably then suggest another venue; lunchtime wine and nibbles, with Helena arriving not at all in the nibbling mood.

I laughed to myself, for I imagined her, standing majestically in her cashmere coat, declaring, as if it were some sort of sexual peccadillo, "I'm sorry, but I don't nibble."

Nibble or not, these friends wanted a good look at this woman who had so mysteriously appeared in my life and they couldn't be put off forever.

As predicted, although having side-stepped the supper engagement with a plausible excuse, I was dismayed at another immediately springing up in its place, described as a 'tastes and teasers' party in celebration of the host's sixtieth birthday. It immediately put me in mind of some seedy gathering, with participants armed with chopsticks selecting tiny specifically shaped savouries off a prone stripogram, but no, it was in fact nothing more than a quiz evening with wine and an assortment of snacks provided.

Reasoning, that in the cut and thrust of such clever-clog's rivalry, Helena's lack of appetite was hardly likely to be noticed and having consulted her, I accepted the invitation. I had first met Jeremy Adams, the birthday boy, a few years previously, prior to him taking early retirement from his high-flying oil executive job. His wife, a little bundle of severity, wrapped in silk, I found rather hard work, but in fairness, she had been his essential aide, majestic at lavish banquets in foreign parts and meticulous when entertaining important guests in whatever outpost they happened to have been stationed. Why they took to me, a frayed collared hobby writer, I never quite figured out. Maybe, it was the fact I was a freer thinker than the local worthies likely to be at the party. Had Jeremy found that refreshing? Who knows, but anyway, I informed Helena of the likely scenario and have to admit it, then felt a frisson building, knowing she'd be at my side.

As it happens, Helena didn't give a flicker of reaction to the upcoming event and on the night in question, wore a simple black dress, pretty off-white crochet cardigan, plus modest gold necklace and tiny black ear studs with diamond centres, that completed the demure look. Any notion of cashmere coated Helena was left within the host's hall cupboard, hanging beside my ancient black overcoat.

I avoided the hot punch, for there was no telling what they'd tipped into it, but Helena partook, while I relished the very good New Zealand and South African white wines on offer, making a mental note of the names, for they were crisp with the lightest of fruit flavours. I'm no wine connoisseur, but dislike white wines, so laden with blended pungency, they almost taste sickly, plus I avoid some of the celebrated reds that are so intense, you'd swear beefsteak had been a solute during maturation.

Hot, delicious offerings were brought through from the kitchen, by a lady dressed in traditional maid's garb and no-one noticed Helena discreetly edging her portions onto my plate. The wicked little minx even said on a couple of occasions, "Oh, you must try this one," before popping it into my mouth.

The quiz itself, covered a broad spectrum, including, historical, geographical, mathematical and scientific in one section; music, films, art and literature in another; TV programmes, media and politics in the third.

There were five couples competing and I won't bore you with the details, other than say, we won. In fact we won, almost to the point of embarrassment, for we didn't get a single answer wrong. Even when asked, 'What would be the first US state encountered when travelling east around the globe from New England?' I, like everyone else assumed it to be Hawaii, but Helena, wrote Alaska, whispering, "The Aleutian Islands span far further west than Hawaii." She was of course right.

Trouble is, it wasn't hard to see we'd overdone it, for the change of mood was almost palpable, swinging from condescension, at such a sweet little thing daring to pit her wits against folk of such venerable wisdom, to finally one of downright resentment, directed not only at Helena, but also at me, for bringing along someone, obviously too clever by half, as if to specifically to steal their thunder. Phew! What a dynamic little package she was turning out to be.

So, not surprisingly, we were first to leave. Jeremy and his wife wore false smiles as they thanked us for coming and following the click of the big front door, I heard the burst of animated chatter. As we scrunched across the gravel, towards my car parked as usual, nose pointing for home, I gave what I guessed would be a final look back at the impressive property. Far side of the spread of light, splayed from the large French windows, I saw shadows behind curtains, moving like puppets in time to the utterances.

Helena drove, as she'd only had the one drink and on the way back, I asked, amongst other things, 'How on earth had she known the answers to questions on British soaps, talent competitions and reality shows?'

"I cheated, darling."

"But how?"

"As the questions were read out, my phone picked them up and relayed the answers."

"But I never saw you look at your phone once."

"No need to," she answered, tapping an earring and flashing a grin.

"You mean they're receptors."

Helena carried on driving.

Chapter Thirteen

The next venue was a rugby club do I'd had an invite to. It involved lunch; being relieved of the usual raffle money in aid of the club; then watching a crunch match between local rivals vying for a position near top of the league, with hope of eventual promotion the following season. Years before I'd have stayed to make a complete night of it, but at my time of life, the thought of endless rounds of beer no longer appealed and so I asked Helena, to please drop me off and then collect me about 5.30pm.

The food was simple fare, soup, followed by beef stew, piles of potatoes and steaming veg, accompanied by almost bearable red wine. As the lemon curd, you could bounce a spoon on, was passed around, the President rose to give a short resume of the club's fortunes, plus gave thanks to all those for attending and as we picked at the cheese and biscuits, conversation centred around England's prospects in the coming six nation's matches, plus of course, there were a good few reminiscences thrown in. The game resulted in a narrow victory for the local lads and so I had a swift couple of pints, to go along with the spirit of things, but was then ready for home.

I was in a group with four others, when all eyes turned to the doorway. Helena, looking snug and glamorous in her cashmere coat, stood peering, trying to locate me.

There were a few comments, nothing too overt of course, but it's best I don't repeat them and leaving my comrades open mouthed, I walked to greet the centre of their attention.

"Am I glad to see you."

"You look fairly well ensconced to me," she replied.

"I just need to say cheerio and then we can leave."

Well you can imagine the speculation regarding the reason for my early departure, but brushing aside such utterances, I just said how great it had been seeing them all again, thanked my friend for the invitation and then turned to leave.

His hand clamped my shoulder. "Now this is all a bit sudden, old chap! Won't do at all," was said in a mock-melodramatic tone, backed up by the other three getting in on the act. Back in my playing days, he had captained the first team for a couple of seasons and hadn't lost his air of authority. "Now we feel, the very least you could do is introduce the lady."

Seeing the others nodding in full agreement, I walked back to the doorway and with a wry look, said, "Sorry Helena, but they would like to meet you."

"Do I have to?"

"It will only take a moment."

Famous last words. Drinks were bought; two wives on a similar mission to Helena's also became embroiled and the whole thing turned into quite a session. It was in fact, immense fun, with avowals to leave shouted down, adding to that magic, when such a gathering burgeons into a small impromptu party.

As the numbers within the clubhouse dwindled, I noticed a few resentful looks from younger members, obviously rather put out, that the oldies were having a better time than they were.

Now here comes the reason for including this little anecdote. When virtually the only ones left in the place, with me feeling pleasantly warmed at seeing how well Helena was getting on with my friends, she suddenly turned and looking close to boiling, mouthed, "So, can we go now?" It truly stunned me, for it was obvious, all her charm and merriment had been merely an act. Luckily no-one had heard and bidding all farewell, I suggested, we'd best ring for a taxi.

"I'm fine," she said, sailing towards the door. We hadn't far to go, it was still fairly early and so I acquiesced. Well let's be truthful, I'd been so shocked by her change of mood I hadn't relished challenging her.

Then with hardly having gone half a mile, a police car overtook with light flashing. It was supposedly just a routine check, but on smelling alcohol, they asked Helena if she had been drinking?

Giving a lady the benefit of the doubt, you might describe her answer as vague, but no matter, they duly breathalysed her.

On examining the result, the officer's face was a picture of puzzlement and that of his colleague was one of obvious annoyance. He did a circuit of the vehicle, examining lights and tyres, asked to see indicators, break lights, windscreen wipers and washers working and on finding nothing at fault, reluctantly waved us on our way.

Once in the clear I asked, "Helena, how on earth did you manage that?"

"Told you I'd be fine."

She did in fact look fine, as if alcohol had no effect on her whatsoever and I commented, "That copper's face was a picture. He couldn't believe his eyes. When he showed his mate, the test kit, I heard him mutter, 'Nothing, zero. It doesn't make sense.'"

Helena's laugh was utterly derisive.

"It seemed as if they had been waiting for us?" I said, hoping some geniality might return.

"No shit, Sherlock!"

'Wherever did she pick up a phrase like that,' I wondered?

Chapter Fourteen

Now, as regards growing old, there is very little to recommend it, especially for a man, for there can come the onset of a paunch, snoring, an annoying frequent need of the bathroom and the more one becomes sensible, the wilder one's eyebrows tend to grow.

There can be a small bonus, however, for if an elderly gent acts perfectly naturally, avoiding any suggestive utterances that might spring to mind, some attractive young ladies can start to behave exactly how a chap wished they'd have done, when back in his youth. In fact, with feeling no sense of threat, the pretty young things can actually become quite flirtatious.

I only write this, because it might help explain what happened one evening after we had returned from a hilltop ramble. It had given me quite an appetite and so wanted to prepare something quick and easy; onions, garlic, mushrooms and thinly sliced carrots, fried in olive oil; a last-minute addition of peas and tinned tuna, before all was added to the boiled rice.

It was one of my tasty stand-by meals and for once Helena, seeing the long grains of rice glistening with interest, said she would try some. I handed her a small portion along with fork and napkin and we sat in the pair of easy chairs chatting, eating and feeling the glow from the Chilean white wine.

I say eating, but Helena had spent more time pushing her food around the plate, rather than consuming any. What she left, I quickly ate in the kitchen, for I hate wasting food and I fished another bottle of wine from out of the fridge.

When topping up Helen's glass, I noticed a tiny stain on her leggings and apologised, for it must have come from the olive oil used in the meal.

"Not to worry, it will soon sponge out," she said and disappeared into the kitchen.

Helena, returning bare footed and wearing nothing but a white blouse, barely long enough, if you know what I mean, smiled and said, "I've left them to dry in the kitchen." Switching off the main light and playfully wagging a finger, she added, "And no looking!"

She settled into the chair opposite and we continued talking in quite a natural fashion, as if conversing with a lady, obviously not wearing knickers, was nothing more than an everyday experience. When a similar scenario had occurred in that hologram episode I mentioned earlier, I had sensed signs of tension, but here, her eyes betrayed a touch of devilment, as if enjoying playing with me.

"I told you, no looking!"

"It's difficult not to, Helena, when you sit like that." I'd obviously wondered, 'Why the removal of underwear?' but was hardly likely to spoil it by asking.

"Why? What's wrong with sitting like this?"

"Well, it's not how ladies normally sit."

Obviously enjoying the situation, she peered down at the slightly tumescent cleft a hand had tilted to prominence and asked, "Is it the depilation that so surprises you?"

I laughed. "Even though it's a bit of an eye opener, Helena, nothing surprises me about you anymore."

Her answer did, however, "I'm doing this, because it's exactly what you want me to do."

I was staggered. "How do you know what goes through a man's mind?"

Giving me a measured look she said, "As you might have noticed, I'm not your average woman."

She certainly wasn't, as had been proven on numerous occasions and with her being such an enigma, it led me to wonder whether the splash of olive oil had been deliberate?

"How do you feel. Sitting here talking like this? Talking to a half-naked lady you've not yet been to bed with."

That word, 'yet,' sent the blood racing and I confessed to the excitement at finding myself in such an unusual scenario, but added, "It all feels quite natural, though, doesn't it? Harming no-one and doing exactly what our instincts tell us."

"You mean, doing exactly what you want me to do."

"You're mind reading again."

"I told you, that's not possible. All that's possible, is the weighing up of possibilities." Then on suddenly remembering, she said, "Oh, and that green tube in the bathroom-----."

"Which green tube, exactly?"

"Yes, I'm sorry. I do seem to have taken the place over. It's the one labelled, 'Silken Care.' Don't ever use it as hair cream."

"I never use hair cream."

Ignoring that, she said laughing, "People will think you've got alopecia." Pondering for a while, Helena gave a wicked look, then added airily, "Even though I've divulged, I'm doing this for your benefit, has it not occurred to you, that a lady might derive equal excitement from such a situation, especially with a certain person showing such obvious appreciation?"

I didn't reply, but simply watched with heart thumping, as Helena stood and then leaning forward, deftly made alterations to my clothing. "There, that's better," she said and sat down again.

My throat had gone dry, but after a slug of wine, I did manage to reply, "Well a man would hope equal excitement would accompany such spirited revelations, but to tell you the truth, no matter how much we would like them to, ladies don't tend to sit in a chair as a you are doing and even if they did, most would be annoyingly coy, instinctively dangling a hand to spare their blushes."

Brightly comfying herself, as if nether regions were still shielded by leggings, she replied, "Now I come to think about it, you're the first man I've ever done this for. As you said, it feels exciting and quite natural, but only if done for the right person. Can you move that lamp, darling?"

I tilted the shade slightly.

"That's it. I like to look while I'm talking to you."

Now you're probably all thinking, this is merely foreplay, leading to a self-gratifying description of a full sexual encounter and if I'd have been younger, it almost certainly would have ended up with both of us in bed, but what you have to remember is, I'm now an old bloke and it had been quite some time since calling the courting tackle into action. What if, when faced with the responsibility of taking advantage of such a momentous opening, it didn't work anymore? We'd had two bottles of wine, with me consuming the lion's share and to have pushed things any further could have easily led to the onset of panic, that fear of failure, at having been called to duty, but then try as one might, coaxing or thrashing it, the glory days lay back in the mists of time, making it no longer possible to rise to the occasion. Then would come the long deafening silence. The immense weight of guilt at having let a lady down, spurning that most treasured gift in her hour of need. In the continuing void, the inner conflict would then commence; my cursing of what had suddenly decided to flop and through gritted teeth, the demand to know, 'Why? **Why**? You know damn well it's what you've always wanted and yet I get a refusal, you blasted thing!'

The inevitable dulcet tones of, "Don't worry, darling," would only increase the pressure, for how can a man not worry when exactly the same thing could happen next time?

No, I decided, an early morning encounter might be wiser and Helena must have realised exactly what was going through my mind, for finally she said, "Look, it's been fun, but I think it's time we both turned in. Would you like me to help get your bed ready?"

"No I can manage thanks."

She was about to mount the stairs, but turning, said, "This will never do. I haven't had my goodnight kiss yet." Approaching, placing one foot directly in front of the other, as if walking a plank, emphasised her femininity and spinning to directly face me, she declared, "Do you realise, you've not yet kissed my lips."

I thought, 'It's not from lack of wanting to,' and there must still be a bit of life in the old dog yet, for a bit of devilment got to me, which caused her to pull away, bending and tugging the hem of her blouse as low as possible. "You *are* naughty, you know!"

"Can't help it Helena. I was born like it."

She leant over and demanded, "Now kiss me properly."

Which I gladly did.

"No, just the once!" she reprimanded and with eyes glinting as if excited by the discovery, Helena repeated, "You really are naughty!"

I of course didn't spoil the charade by pointing out she'd been the instigator of the whole affair and with a thrill tingling right through my body, found it a struggle to get to sleep that night, for I now knew what was going to happen, but didn't know when exactly.

Chapter Fifteen

The worst of winter seemed to be over and even though occasional snow flurries still wet our faces when on countryside rambles, we knew it was just 'lamb's wool' and the grim ruler of the dark times had been defeated for yet another year.

Often when we walked towards *our* bridge, I expected Helena to say, pointing up into the woods, 'That's where I lost my phone,' but she never did and I never told her, that's where I had found it. Why, you might ask? Well, she was such a strange enigmatic little package, it sometimes made me feel vulnerable with a need to keep something in reserve.

'Some hope,' you might say, and yes I know how like putty men can be in the hands of a pretty lady, but I was doing my best. Now, here's another secret. I didn't let on about the books I'd had published. More of a hobby really and didn't relish the thought, she might bring a cold splash of reality, by saying, 'Well, they're not bad.'

On our wanderings we covered all sorts of topics, the conversation dancing freely and sometimes, when out in the car, our destination would arrive that abruptly, I realised I'd not noticed any of the usual landmarks along the way. We hadn't built up to this mutual understanding in a slow, getting to know one another, sort of fashion, it had happened instantly, like the flick of a switch and now we even had a history. 'Remember that bloke in the frock?' Or, 'Do you remember that night we went badger watching?'

It was a simple encounter in a supermarket, however, that really brought it home to me what had happened. The full emotional depth I had arrived at. It was the type of outlet that's not the best for a full weekly shop, but it did stock, along with a few staples, interesting items from right around the globe. My task had been quite simple, just seeking out the herb and spice section, but I'd asked Helena if she could locate a particularly delicious relish from the Adriatic region, called Ajvar. It was red-pepper based, with a piquancy that acts as a perfect accompaniment to sausages and of course the J is pronounced as a Y.

I had found what I was looking for and I don't know why it is, but when certain ladies are espied from out of the corner of an eye, it can bring a slight jolt from within, followed by the compulsion to look fully at the cause of the sensation.

I found myself gazing directly at Helena and from that point on, knew there was no going back, for I'd fallen hopelessly in love. If there had been a heat imaging camera in the store, my body would have been glowing like a beacon, which just goes to show, you don't necessarily need sex to find yourself thus ensnared.

Now we come to the bit you're not going to believe, but please do, for it actually happened. Listen to this. One night, completely out of the blue, Helena came back downstairs and suggested we cuddle for a while in my bed. In fact, shivering, she clung to me like a limpet and so obviously felt the immediate reaction it brought. Other than say, my hands caressing her breasts, thighs and vagina had found all slightly swollen and fully receptive, as if anticipating the coming prospect, I'm not going into further detail. Out of respect for the lady and the fact it's all been described countless times before, I'm afraid I must leave it to your imagination.

You're going to need it, mind you, if you've any hope of keeping up with this next bit.

As we clung together, I felt a rush within, surging with such intensity, I'm sure it would have eclipsed anything certain drugs are said to do to the system, for I experienced the sensation of us flying together at breakneck speed as if aboard a crazy devilish machine, but then realised, it wasn't like some out of control will-o'-the-wisp, for as mad as it seems, Helena was somehow handling where we flew, taking us this way and that, wild mistress of the skies. I was completely at her mercy, for as we soared up through clouds and screamed back towards earth, pulling out of near-death dives, leaving my brain blacked out and stomach behind, I could almost hear her screeching with glee inside my head. It was both terrifying and exhilarating and my whole body trembled as I clung on, almost sick with fear.

The journey continued barely above wave tops and I swear I could smell the brine and feel spray on my legs; then as we leisurely patrolled above palms and huts, brown skinned natives looked up and pointed. Open mouthed, they watched as we zoomed off again, soaring through clouds to where the dazzling sun lit up tumultuous columns of gathering storms.

In my mind Helena was laughing, sharing the ecstasy of our crazy loops and weaves over land and sea and as she pointed out various locations, words weren't needed for she was inside me, sharing my body. To be almost chemically bonded with this person who had captured my heart, believe me, it bettered anything of a sexual nature. It felt like, for the first time in my life, my eyes had been fully opened, as if offering a conversion and access to another world, plus the privileged sensation of feeling different to every other living being. Had I crossed over into a secret twilight zone where none could follow?

The next morning, when awaking, I wondered whether I'd simply dreamt the whole thing. My body felt slightly fatigued, but also, from deep within came a sense of rejuvenation as if emerging from a deep curative sleep. Checking beneath the covers I almost expected to see damp and debris, evidence of our wild adventure, but of course all was normal, for apart from a certain deed, I spared you the details of, all had been entirely in the mind.

When Helena finally descended, wearing a grin as impish as a pixie, I knew the whole thing hadn't been entirely personal and merely a dream, but how had she managed it?

"Managed what exactly?"

"You know what I mean. I didn't dream it. Somehow we were flying together with our minds almost joined as one."

"Oh, that!" She gave a wicked look and said, "Magic."

"No please, Helena. It was the weirdest experience of my life."

"Did I scare you?"

"I'll say you did. On a number of occasions, I really thought we were goners."

"What! Don't you trust me?"

"Yes, but how did you do it."

"It's just the phone, silly. I can get it to do all sorts of things."

I shook my head, "This is beyond belief, Helena. I know phones have the amazing capacity to store data, translate and give instant answers off the internet, but I've never heard of a flying phone before."

"Well as they say, there's a first time for everything."

It was at this point, I couldn't help it and must apologise for being a silly old fool, for I pulled her into an embrace and confessed I was in love with her.

Was it a dangerous thing to do, leaving me entirely vulnerable? I didn't care, for besotted as any teenager,

I had become completely smitten. Didn't tell her where I'd found that phone mind you. And don't go mentioning those books I told you about.

'So who's a big strong boy then?' you might think.

As we went about the day's tasks and then later, for a walk, I noticed I had a greater reserve of energy and felt more lithe in my movements. When resting, mid-afternoon on low grass banking, I didn't feel the creak of knees when easing myself down and then when rising again, managed it without a laborious turn sideways, to push myself up by use of both hands. It made me gasp in wonder, as if slowly being freed from the bonds of old age. I have to admit, I was so elated, I almost gave the simple act of sitting down, another go.

Later, I managed to resist the compulsion of giving Helena a quick kiss on the cheek in the coffee shop, I hate seeing mature couples canoodling and didn't want to sicken others with the sight, but I tell you what, you've no idea how close I came to grabbing her in an ecstatic squeeze and couldn't wait for what the coming evening might have in store.

We never really know though do we and when trying to put myself in Helena's position, I felt a sudden discomfiture at what she may have now been thinking; 'I didn't mind this relationship, when on my terms, but with him now having fallen in love, it changes everything. All getting a bit too heavy,' so to speak.

Then a surge of panic suddenly took me. What if she's thinking, 'He's now likely to be a flaming pest, constantly asking why I've gone so quiet, repeatedly asking if I'm happy, or wanting to know what I'm thinking? What if he starts following me everywhere, enquiring, 'Where are you going now?' If he starts following me to the lavatory, I swear I'll scream!'

As we drove home, I recalled once being in the very same situation as Helena, for I'd unintentionally caused a lady to fall in love with me, making her so impossibly clingy it had made me feel overwhelmed and trapped. I decided to ease back a bit on the 'silly old duffer in love' stuff and give Helena some breathing space.

"You're very quiet," she said.

"I'm still stunned by what happened last night."

With a sigh she said, "We won't play that same game tonight. Takes too much out of me," but then, giving my arm a squeeze, added, "I'll still come to your bed though, just for a cuddle. That's if you want me to."

Want her to? With heart soaring I said, "Helena, of course I want you to."

"Keep your eyes on the road, dear."

As we drove on in silence, I mulled over her confession, that the strange mind-numbing experience of seemingly having taken part in a wild video game, had taken too much out of her. Not out of the phone battery, but out of her. I could hardly take the point up, though, could I?

That would have really ruined everything and I had prospect of the coming evening to look forward to.

As promised, she came to my bed for, shall we call it a cuddle? The same happened on the following two evenings, but she was a clever little thing and on the final morning said, "I think I'm wearing you out. Would it be best if we kept to our own beds tonight?"

At a pretence of virility, I took slight issue with the notion, but then agreed and put the linen from both beds in the wash. Clean sheets would aid a good night's sleep and I tell you what; I actually began to look forward to easing between their crisp, cool cleanliness, like a balm to my worn-out body.

Helena's company had certainly had that rejuvenating effect on me, but I don't know if most men are the same when getting on in years, for I found that after having had enough of what I'd been longing for, my mind would then start to tell me, 'That's enough of that for a while, old fella, you need a rest.'

For women it's different of course, for even if they might not be in the mood for further activity of a sexual nature, straight after having already done it, there's nothing actually stopping their equipment from doing it all again, immediately. Most men, however, need a rest, until something triggers a reaction. No good forcing it and it could be just the simplest of gestures that fires it up again, but without that loving smile, stroke of hand or nuzzle, you could will the thing all you liked, but it still wouldn't work. Also, if a woman is too forceful, thinking a damn good pumping will revive it, the opposite happens, bringing on the equivalent of boozer's droop.

Now, remember me telling you, I suspected Helena could read my mind, well I don't think such a gift was required following the three-night fallow period.

We were in a fond embrace in the kitchen, when looking up she said, "Hey, I know what you're after."

"Am I that easy to read?"

"Of course, apart from anything else, your eyes begin to get that glazed look."

She was right of course. I could have pulled her knickers down there and then, but decided it would be wiser to wait and I'm very glad I did.

As before, I won't trouble you with the most intimate details, but will instead move swiftly on to post erotic activities.

The afternoon was hot, the cicadas were almost deafening, the air aromatic with herbs and from our high vantage point, we could see the distant sparkle of the sea.

Suddenly all went silent.

"Something's happened," said Helena and pushing me off the cliff, she called, "Let's take a look."

In sheer terror, I plummeted headlong towards distant rocks, but then felt the unbelievable relief of Helena's embrace, halting my descent. "Lean towards the sea, "she said. "That's it, we should just about make it."

Well the fact is, it became obvious that we couldn't and so Helena, pointing to a large swimming pool, yelled in my ear, "Get ready for splashdown."

I could actually feel us plunge with the bubbles to the bottom and then when rising with the sun dazzling through water-filled eyes, I espied, of all people, Jeremy Adams sitting amongst his pals.

"Glad you could both drop in," he said, as we hauled ourselves out. "We were discussing that ludicrous one-way system they've just installed. It means that if you drive in from College Street with the Royal on your right, you have to go right round the flaming town just to get to the hotel entrance."

I looked at him mouth agape. Here we were in some exotic far-flung setting and they were all still fixating on boring details of home.

"Did you hear about that traffic warden none of us like? He's got done for stealing lady's knickers off a neighbour's washing line."

"Fascinating," I said, but if you'll excuse us, Helena thinks something massive has just happened out at sea.

As we left, I muttered, "Helena, how did you bring them into the story? This is unreal."

"I know, but isn't it fun."

She eased us aloft again and we could see a huge wall of water surging towards land. It was a tsunami of such magnitude, it made beach front villas and palm trees look as if mere toys.

Gliding down we alighted outside a bar, that crowded, many customers had spilled onto the pavement and apart from a few tiny ladies of possible oriental origin, all were men, wearing white shirts, designer jeans, slip-on shoes and the most apt collective noun I could think of, was a swagger.

Helena tried desperately to shout a warning of imminent death, but then turning to me, said aghast, "They won't listen!"

"Of course not, Helena, they're bankers. Too busy talking about themselves. Somehow, you've managed to bring a swagger of bankers into the story.

She laughed in that way she had, making me want to hug her, but no, we took flight again floating along the sea front, where countless numbers of what looked like students, all had that furtive hunched look of hoodies, but minus the hoods, for they were all were intently bent over phones. We tried pushing a few into a run to escape, but it was useless. After a few stuttering steps, they'd stop, to animatingly thumb their phones again.

With the water now a deafening thunder we took off just as it surged through the streets taking all before it. Other waves followed finishing the demolition of the town. Bodies floated back and forth like shoals of dead fish, but

I noticed as we swooped low inland, a few survivors lay stranded, the only sign of life being thumbs; frantically flicking on dead phones like crabs' antennae.

Again, when I awoke I was alone. I had that rejuvenated feeling that had been so prevalent after our previous flight of fantasy and on a moment of inspiration, I risked doing five press-ups. Not so long back, I'd not even have managed to push myself off the floor. I had a cup of tea and a meagre breakfast, then waited. On suddenly remembering a few annoying financial details that needed sorting, I used the idle time to get the task done, then having finished and still no sign of life, I thought it best to go up and see if Helena was alright.

Tapping on the door, I whispered her name, but got no answer. I pushed the door open and saw she was still asleep, flat on her back. As witnessed once before, the wire to charge her phone led up under the covers, but as I turned to leave, I spotted something that sent a shock wave through my system of such magnitude, I'm surprised it didn't awaken her.

On the bedroom chair lay her phone, completely alone, without any sign of it being recharged.

As I crept downstairs my heart was pounding and going into the cool of the kitchen, tore off two sheets of paper towel, for I was sweating profusely. Returning to the parlour, I sat down, then got up again, then pacing the room asked myself, "What was that wire recharging?" I know it's wicked of me to think this, but I actually hoped it had been connected to some sexual device, but instincts told me it hadn't.

When Helena finally descended, she stretched and said, "What a sleep." Then peering, asked, "What's the matter, darling? It looks as if you've seen a ghost."

Once again, she refused any breakfast, saying her little white tablets sufficed and of course, all our conversation was about the previous night's adventure. I told her I had been absolutely petrified, thinking she had pushed me to my death and asked, how had she managed such a perfect image of Jeremy Adams? It had been that real, if I were to meet him in town later, I'd feel compelled to ask how he'd got back so quickly, for only hours earlier I'd seen him, large as life, reclining by a foreign swimming pool.

When I tried to dig deeper, asking how it had all been possible and so vivid, I was again fobbed off with the phone story. Of course, everything inside me wanted to believe her, plus there was that other reason for swallowing the line, for if I admitted I'd seen her earlier with the phone lead nowhere near the instrument in question, it could well have invited that other Helena onto the scene, the one as frosty as an ice queen and so I held back, suggesting we go out for the day.

Yes, I realised I was taking the path of least resistance, but why spoil a promising day? But there again, try as I might, I couldn't get that vision out of my mind, of Helena laid out like a corpse and that phone lead plugged into Lord knows what. I was being weak, I admit that, but didn't want to invite the loss of such a treasure that had come to me so late in life.

Of course, this is how certain ladies work. I'd been around long enough to know that; for if their command is challenged, then look out, for if you are reckless enough to summon the dragon or whatever other alter ego lurks, it's hardly their fault if it duly appears. Some work it differently, feigning sudden illness if they can't get their own way. Men will never fully understand them.

So not wishing to invite the ice queen out for the day, I kept a wise council and we chatted about all sorts of things, but eventually ended up talking about previous partners. Not in detail, I hasten to add, just the main reasons why various liaisons hadn't worked. Must admit, I did most of the probing, as I was baffled as to why such an attractive woman was still single. I could tell she'd not had children by the way, and it's hard to explain how exactly, but fathering a son and daughter must have somehow bestowed on me a different aura and understanding compared to those who are childless.

As Helena ran through a few anecdotes, of how a number of extremely wealthy gentlemen had lavished fabulous jewellery and gifts on her and had wined and dined her in the most exclusive places, I didn't feel jealous, for as she explained how she'd eventually had to disappoint every one of them, I was actually made to feel like a confidant. There again, experience had shown me, the cleverest trick a con artist pulls, is to explain exactly how they'd managed such amazing deceptions, without the listener realising they were being lined up as the next victim. But Helena could hardly be conning me. How could she? Compared to her previous partners I was a relative pauper, which brought me back to that nagging question, 'Why me?'

The main destination that day was a vineyard, where a small café served quite tasty local fare and we both opted for the soup which was delicious, as was my home baked bread. The wine was pricey, but I always try to support local enterprises and as soon as we got back, popped both bottles into the fridge. It would be the perfect end to a pleasant day. Or so I thought.

All went well to start with, but emboldened by the wine and even though instinctively knowing it was stupid of me, I enquired about the phone lead I'd seen that morning.

"It was charging the phone, silly."

"But the phone wasn't in bed with you."

"Well of course not. I didn't want to roll on it and so put it on the side."

I know I should have left it there, but said, "But the phone wasn't on the bedside table, Helena, it was on the chair across the other side of the room."

"Table, chair, what's the difference? I hope you're not going to come snooping *every* morning!"

"I wasn't snooping. You'd been in bed so long, I was simply worried in case you weren't well."

All I got in reply was a glare. That's until I artlessly added, "Well it *is* my bedroom. Helena."

"Oh I see! If you don't want me here, I can soon sort that out!"

"No, Helena----" but too late, she was off upstairs.

I awoke the following morning, half expecting to find that she had slipped away in the night, but no she was there alright, or a version of her was, cold as ice. Any attempt at conversation was completely ignored and on the trip into town for supplies, she happily chatted to the grocer and butcher, as if to highlight the rift between us, but once back in the car, was completely unapproachable.

I won't bore you too much with it, but suffice to say, the cold shoulder treatment went on for two whole days, until I felt like the loneliest man in the world, inside my own house. In fact, the neighbour's cat got more attention than I did.

On the third day, expecting Helena to tell me she was leaving, she came downstairs, bright as a button as if nothing had happened. I couldn't believe it. As if by a simple click of a switch I had my darling Helena back, but where had the ugly sister gone? Had she been left in the wardrobe, or was she still lurking inside the person standing before me? Also, the most troubling question was, which was the real Helena? Was it the one I had fallen in love with, or had that version been nothing but a clever act? And yet again, I asked myself, 'Why me?'

I would like to be able to tell you everything ran smoothly from hereon, but sadly it didn't. Something had changed and I didn't quite know what. Helena would often seem distant and actually, slightly troubled, which was a thing I hadn't expected. We still went to various destinations when the weather permitted, but it felt like a vital spirit had departed, leaving behind no more than a vague shell.

In the end, when I felt compelled to ask her, what was the matter, I got the, 'Nothing. Please don't fuss,' reply. Then one day, when I finally dared believe I had my Helena back, two small dogs went absolutely berserk as we entered a pub for lunch, making such a hysterical racket, we had to go straight back out again. By the time we reached the next decent food outlet, the kitchen had stopped serving and even though it would hardly have mattered to Helena, I was so ravenous I devoured a packet of crisps along with a pickled egg.

When I did finally manage to prise some sort of answer from her, Helena confessed, she had been called. It seemed a strange term, one you'd associate with the priesthood, a calling from above, but I assumed it meant, her services were further required in the diplomatic service. On being asked when she was to be called exactly, I just received an infuriating shrug in reply, but didn't press the issue as that drawn, lank haired look was returning as if badly ailing from something within.

Well of course, for me it was like walking on eggshells, plus I had the added fear she would just slip away in the night, as done previously. I'm lucky that one of my old school mates was still alive to share my troubles with. Also of course I'd poured my heart out somewhat, to my children. My son had been very concerned, warning me, he didn't like the sound of it and to be careful, while my daughter said, she reminded her of the phantom in

Greek mythology, the Lamia, who seduced men before devouring them, or in some versions, was a voluptuous woman with a serpent's tail.

Anyway, as I explained the situation to my old mate Joe, I could hear him laughing that heartily on the end of the line, it sounded like he was on the verge of gaining a damp patch.

"You mean to tell me, you stumble on a phone in the woods, and when you answer it, it leads to this right cracker, half your age?"

"Steady on Joe, she's not that young."

"OK, but it still means, that when out on nothing more than a bit of a ramble, a lost phone leads you to this woman of your dreams."

"Well, I suppose so, yes."

"And now you tell me, she's living with you."

"Well not exactly. She has her own room."

"But you've only got the one bedroom and that space you use as a store."

"I know."

"So where do you sleep?"

"Downstairs."

He burst out laughing. "You mean she's swanning around upstairs while you kip on the sofa?"

I had to wait awhile for the mirth to abate. "Not exactly. I have a sofa bed."

"And what about your clothes? Do you have to make an appointment to get dressed?"

"No, she thought it would benefit us both, if I took the bulk of my things downstairs."

"Dear God! At this rate she'll have you living out in the tool shed."

"No, Joe. I know things are a bit tricky at the moment, but when she's in one of her better moods, you couldn't wish for better company."

"Are you quite sure you've checked all your lottery numbers? I reckon you've won the jackpot, but don't realise it?"

"No, you've got it wrong, Joe. She's not the grasping type."

"Come off it! She's heard you've got a pension increase coming. She's after your extra 15 quid a week, mate."

His laughter was infectious and also pierced straight through the strange scenario I'd allowed to develop. It had all happened in what seemed like logical steps, but standing back from what it had finally become, I had to agree, it was undeniably weird.

"Now tell me again about all this flying stuff," he chortled.

When I did, he said, "You're having me on. You haven't been flying. She's been slipping you a Micky Finn, mate. Do you know if she takes drugs of any sort?"

I told him about the lack of eating and mysterious white pills, to which he suggested I post him a couple. A mate of his would run them through a lab test.

He thanked me for the call and was just about to go, when obviously a last-minute thought struck, "Hey! D'you----?"

"What?"

"Look, I know she's a bit weird,----but d'you give her one?"

"Joe--!"

"Well, it's not like I'm asking for details."

"We have become quite close, Joseph."

"Well that's something I suppose. Send me a couple of those pills."

It seemed like a treacherous thing to do, but there again, I felt I deserved some answers. The chat with him, woke me up rather and straight away, Helena could sense something had changed.

"You've been a long time."

"I was just chatting to an old mate of mine."

As I put the few things I'd bought, inside the fridge, I heard, "What about?"

"Oh, just this and that."

The look she gave, brought my daughter's word to mind, Lamia.

It wasn't difficult to obtain a couple of the white pills, for she kept them in an old-fashioned silver purse. I had the feeling, time was of the essence, for Helena's movements had become more urgent of late and she had the restlessness of a bird about to migrate. The tension was building to such an extent, I began to wish she would just get on with it, for with her yet again seeming so distant, I felt a morbid loneliness whilst living within my own house. Well, I say living, it was more like existing through an endless state of limbo, with the added insult of the neighbour's cat looking so flaming smug each time it made an appearance.

We did still venture out, but it's not worth giving you the details, other than regarding one strange occurrence. We were on our way home and I remembered there was no bread in the house and we were running short of milk. I stopped at a store run by a charming Indian family. Both their children had left home, one being a Mister in the medical profession and the other an architect, meaning when the present shop owners retired, that would probably be the end of the store.

I hadn't been in there for some time and couldn't believe the difference, for it was like entering a beleaguered outpost, with iron grills protecting window and door, plus more guarding the counter. All high value items were beyond reach and there was a lock on the fridge containing alcohol. Mr. Patel the shopkeeper, explained that theft had become such an everyday occurrence, it was fast becoming uneconomical to continue. He had repeatedly phoned the police, telling them he had CCTV footage of the culprits, but they had done precisely nothing.

Helena seemed to snap out of her recent malaise to offer the man a few words of genuine sympathy and we were just about to leave, when two men wearing covid masks burst through the door. They stared around in desperation, looking for something worth stealing and then one, spotting Helena's handbag, made a lunge for it.

It all happened too quickly to describe, other than say he ended up writhing on the floor and when his accomplice made a dash for the door, something zapped him that hard, he fell flat on his back, to jerk alarmingly like a dying fish.

Mr. Patel thanked us, but then ushered us to the door, "You must make haste. You must not dilly-dally, the police will be taking this very seriously."

He was right, it was on the local news that night. The police were on the lookout for a couple who had put two suspected shoplifters in hospital. Obviously, Mr. Patel hadn't revealed my identity, but I would be there large as life if they bothered to go through CCTV footage and then they'd come asking, what exactly had happened. Had Helena tasered them? I'd seen no sign of any such device, nor that famous phone of hers. So how had she done it? She wouldn't tell me and when I could see her getting thoroughly annoyed, I gave up asking.

Not surprisingly, the worry of this strange power Helena possessed, kept me up half the night and I was still mulling it over for much of the following morning. Finally, looking at my watch, I thought, 'She seems to be in need of an inordinate amount of sleep,' and went up to see if she was alright. The bed was neatly made and there on the pillow, was a note.

"You know I hate long goodbyes, darling. I've left you my spare phone. When I call, set it up like we did before, Helena. X"

Part Four

Chapter Sixteen

Even when you know a person's departure is inevitable, nothing really prepares you for that feeling of devastation when it actually happens. Even the bedroom had that hollow feeling and opening the wardrobe, I realised why. All Helena's clothes had gone. I looked in the chest of drawers, under the bed and even in the bathroom, but all trace of her had vanished. Picking up her note again, I gazed longingly at the X at the end, trying to read more into it than there actually was; a mere sweetening of the bitter truth; Helena had left me.

I rang my daughter, who immediately insisted I go and stay with them in Devon for a few days and quickly packing I left early afternoon. Even though of course, blocked from using the phone Helena had left, I still took it with me. It was the main remaining link to her and if a call came through, I presumed the green button would still allow me to answer.

I felt so completely numb, I don't remember much about the journey. My daughter, Hannah was there to greet me, but my son in law was out working late. I crept upstairs for a peep at my grandson, fast asleep in his bed.

Hannah rustled up a quick snack and then asked whether I needed a nap after the long journey? When I said, no, I could tell by the way she approached, she was going to plonk herself in my lap, just as she used to do when a little girl. Hugging me tight, she said, "Oh dad, I'm so sorry. This shouldn't be happening to you."

My poor darling girl was almost crying on my behalf. When she had recovered, she sat beside me on the sofa and asked me to go through everything again from the start.

She was a good listener, only interrupting to clear up a few details I'd not made clear and at the end of the sorry saga, she declared, "Dad, this just doesn't make sense. Why would an attractive woman, in her mid-forties, go for my dad, whose been long retired?"

"I'm not that bad surely."

"Course not. You look nothing like your age, but even so, you have to admit, it's a bit weird."

"That's what Joe said."

"And you say she doesn't eat."

"The odd bowl of cereal or soup, but mainly gets by on those magic tablets I told you about."

"Magic tablets? Rubbish! I'm sorry to say it, dad, but she's been taking you for a fool. In fact, her leaving has done you a favour. You might not think so now, but give it time and you'll realise you've had a lucky escape. From what you tell me, you could have been electrocuted in your own bed."

"No the sofa bed, Han."

"Dear me, dad!" she said laughing. "Of course, we all wanted you to be happy, but seems to me, you've been led a bit of a dance."

We sat in silence for a while and then with a puzzled look, she asked, "Can you describe again what happened on that quiz evening?"

I did so, explaining the role of the phone and earring receptors, to which Hannah said, "It all sounds a bit fishy to me. In fact, she almost sounds like a machine, herself."

I laughed. "Anyone who could concoct a machine that lifelike would be a multi-millionaire."

"No dad," she said with a serious shake of the head. "The whole thing just doesn't add up. There's a piece missing and I can't figure out what it is."

The week in Devon helped me get over some of the heartache, but I simply dreaded the return to my empty house. We went for walks over the moors, taking in turns to carry my grandson, wrapped up warm in the backpack. At streams and pools we let him explore, but kept a keen eye on the little chap, for water of any description acted like a magnet.

Hannah was very good, listening to yet more details of my strange affair and when I said, "I bet you're sick of hearing about it," she replied, that no it was good, acting like a therapy, getting it off my chest.

As for the phone, on examining it, she pronounced it to be as weird as Helena sounded and suggested I fling the thing in the river. I was tempted, but that would be the main link with Helena gone. It lay dormant all that week, by the way.

One evening, we were kindly given a meal by Hannah's in-laws and on another, they baby sat while we went out for a pub meal. My son in law was in good form and even though Hannah had warned I might not be the life and soul, none of his friends probed into my recent demise.

They were all very pleasant, but there was something a little brittle about the ladies in our company. When I dared say to Hannah, next day, that I had noticed something stiff and unnatural, she laughed and suggested I get out more. "Don't you realise, Dad? They're all on Botox. They're all at it. Getting peppered with injections. It's costing them a fortune."

"But it's like a mask. Frightened of smiling in case they crack it."

"They're all scared of growing old."

"But hasn't the fact dawned, it's making them old inside? Personality deadened by self-obsession. And as for that prim blonde one! She looked like she'd been given a good backhander in the mouth!"

Hannah burst out laughing and said, "I think I can see my old dad returning."

Chapter Seventeen

On returning home, luckily, I found a parking space near the house, but my heart immediately sank at the sight of litter in the garden. As I forced the door open past the junk mail, the neighbour's cat brushed past me, going straight upstairs and thinking it might know something I didn't, I followed. Disappointment; the bedroom was as empty as I'd left it and the cat, with an accusing look, leapt off the bed with a thud and went back downstairs.

Being a Saturday I thought I'd better get some supplies in, but the next day took the bold step of knocking on my neighbour's door, for I wondered whether he or his wife could shed any light on how Helena had decamped in such a clandestine manner. You know how things can nag away at you. I half expected to be told, a chauffeur driven limousine had arrived to collect all her belongings, for she was now in the arms of some multi-millionaire yacht owner.

A waft of grease and old socks hit me as the door was eased open. "So there you are," said my neighbour. "They've been looking for you."

"Who exactly?"

"The law of course."

I feigned total ignorance and although hating to be in need of his help, asked whether either he or his wife had seen packing cases, or articles of clothing being taken from my house?"

"No good asking me squire, that new job of mine has me out, dawn 'til dusk. Hang on, I'll ask the missus. BERYL!"

His dumpy wife bustled to the door and on hearing my enquiry answered, "Isn't it dreadful."

"Sorry, what is dreadful?"

"All those trees they've chopped down in Lime Avenue." She looked truly aghast. "All done in the blink of an eye. I used to love walking down there of an autumn day. We both did, didn't we Cliff?"

In all fairness to Cliff, he wore a look of, 'What?'

"They'll be chopping these down next. Flaming criminal. They go on about saving the planet, then chop the bleedin' trees down."

"But our good neighbour wants to know," said Cliff patiently, "did you notice anyone recently, carting away goods and chattels from his house?"

"Oh him! That skinny bloke. Yes I saw him. He was here at least twice. Strange looking blighter."

"Thank you," I said. "Thank you very much. That's been a great help." As I entered my house, I heard Beryl say to her husband. "That fancy piece of his was helping him. Told you it would end in tears."

If that wasn't bad enough, early the next morning an officer of the law appeared.

He asked, could he enter the house and then informed me of the subject of particular interest. Confirming I was definitely the taller of the two individuals, captured on CCTV whilst in Mr. Patel's establishment on the day two young frequenters had been incapacitated, I was requested to give details of what had happened and of course divulge the identity of the shorter of the two personages evident in the retrieved film. On the latter matter, he was obviously far from satisfied and so tried various approaches, only to come back to the fact and I'll put it in normal English, I had let a lady stay in my house without really knowing where she had come from and hadn't even taken the trouble to ask her, her surname. Well of course, he just wouldn't let the matter rest, but with having told all I knew countless times, I became so infuriated, I found myself on the verge of requesting, he put himself on the far side of my front door.

Then when he asked for my definition of, 'Zap,' as in what had befallen the two would-be thieves, I reached for the dictionary and suggested he look the word up for himself, listed under Z. But it was his request to look round the rest of the house, that really got under my skin. Here I was, feeling totally bereft; he knew this, I'd stupidly told him and yet he still expected me to allow him to go tramping over my property, poking into cupboards and personal belongings. Gritting my teeth, I told him once again, every trace of Helena had gone and I was afraid he'd have to take my word for it. Tiny lie of course. I still had the phone.

He reluctantly rose to go, saying there might be a need for him to return.

"I'm afraid, you'll be wasting police time. There's nothing more I can tell you."

Before finally leaving, he told me the two suspected shoplifters were still in a bad way and then with an effort at chumminess, said the Patels had been elated by the outcome, as they'd had no more thefts since the incident. I thanked him for the information, but still couldn't take to the man. In fact, I found his attempt at friendliness more unnerving than his professional persona.

I don't know about you, but I find it infuriating that the perfect line often occurs when the opportunity to say it has slipped by. "If you'd have answered the Patel's calls, on all those occasions they were being robbed, this might never have happened!" But, no. The police car went gliding past, the corner of the lace curtain next door fell back into place and I shut the front door, regretting I'd not been sharp enough to deliver the retort.

My avowal that Helena had disappeared without a trace, was in fact untrue on two counts. First, of course I still had her phone, but second; I couldn't believe how much of her hair I'd found. It was as if it had been left to mock me. I diligently hoovered the place, but still came across numerous strands and the sink and shower took the best part of an hour before finally flushing the last of it down the lavatory. I was amazed she hadn't gone bald.

I gradually began to ease myself back into some sort of routine and found that making lists helped. It was a sort of mental game. Each evening I'd compile a list of tasks for the following day and no matter how much I hated the thought of undertaking certain duties, if they were on the list, they had to be done. Of course, there came that slight elation when a nasty little matter was resolved, but sometimes the whole process of what had seemed like a simple task could end up so frustratingly tortuous, it would become worthy of relating as an anecdote.

Well you all know what it's like. Dealing with some queries can waste half a day. You can be on the phone, pressing this and that number as the options come up, to then be told, proof is required that it's actually you ringing. 'A code will be sent to your phone for you to tap in for verification.' Of course, when you look for it, contact is lost with whatever you were initially connected to. So back you go to, 'All our operatives are busy right now. Your call is important to us. We are experiencing much higher than normal, etc.'

Then I'd think, 'I bet Helena could sort this out in no time.' You've no idea how much I missed her.

One task that wasted half a morning, was enquiring why my electricity bill was more than double the amount it should have been. When I finally got some sense on the matter, I found they hadn't made a mistake at all, for somehow I'd used enough power to have recharged an electric vehicle every night.

A horrifying thought struck, 'Helena!!' The image returned of her laid out like a corpse, with an electric charging cable leading up under the bedclothes.

If that wasn't bad enough, my mate Joe rang, saying the results were back, regarding the tablets I'd sent him.

"Flour and water, mate."

"Surely not."

"'Afraid so. Practically no nutritional value at all. My mate said, the flour had come from some rarified grain, possibly one of those Turkish strains, but even so, there's no way a person could survive on them."

I told him that Helena had left and I was busy trying to piece my life back together. He took roughly the same stance as my daughter, "I think you'll find she's done you a favour. Didn't like to say at the time, but the whole thing sounded more than just weird. Ominous in fact. Couldn't see any good coming from it at all."

"Thanks Joe. Can't help it though. I feel like I've lost part of my body."

"I tell you what. If things get too bad, give me a ring. We'll book up a blokes' weekend away. No women sticking their oar in. We'll go back to one of the old haunts, have some decent grub, a good laugh and maybe even quaff a little alcohol."

"Thanks Joe, you're a good mate. I feel better already."

That was until the nighttime. The fact that I'd never before, got on with a woman so instantly and intensely, constantly haunted, leaving me turning one way, then the other, unable to sleep. I almost began to feel ill from it.

I'm not going to go on about it though, far from me to bore others. There again, I'd better tell you this bit. For some reason, my mind had become racked by memories of ladies I'd met; initially attractive, like sirens captivating as if ideal partners, until they'd spent extensive time under my roof. The two who had done counselling courses turned out to be the most exasperating. It actually became impossible to hold a conversation with either, for no matter what the subject, each felt compelled to scotch any further discussion with, something like, "Well, that's because-----etc." Or if I attempted garnering interest by describing something particularly funny or bizarre, it would be dismissed with a shrug, followed by, "Well of course, you will find this is normal."

It wasn't even possible to share the frustration felt, at being unable to speak to an actual person regarding a bank matter, or to express disgust at what some supermarkets dished up: fruit, rock hard until rotten; strawberries, tomatoes and cucumbers, great to look at, but bereft of flavour; tasteless spongy bread, sour oranges-----. After a moment's deliberation would come a pronouncement along the lines of, "Well you say that, but have you ever thought, it could be the same in other countries?"

"Look! I just want to talk to you. I'm not expecting the wisdom of some 'effin' Solomon!"

"Well there's no need to be like that."

I mustn't go on. Well just one more and then I'll stop. The conversation stealer. Half way through a sentence, explaining the frustration of trying to find an address while driving alone through South Kensington, one could be left open mouthed at hearing something like, "Well I wouldn't do that! In fact, when Ron and I were out in Malta---"

As said, I'd be left, gawping and wondering, 'How the hell did we suddenly end up in Valetta?'

However, providing Helena was not in one of her prickly moods, she could be fun, with conversation flowing easily as water. The loss was made all the worse by the knowledge, I'd never find her like again.

Then that same copper turned up, saying he needed to take a statement. I noticed as he wrote, he had very clean, manicured nails. I read it through and signed it. He told me, I could well be receiving a request to come to the station.

"How kind," I said and closed the door.

Because such a love in my life had gone, all the inefficiencies of our country seemed magnified. Transport services cancelled, train drivers on strike, doctors and nurses on strike, shop staff not having a clue about what they were selling and if you complained it was taken as abuse. Even in the local bakery, where one could at least buy proper bread, the teenage shop girls would go into a fit of nervous giggles if asked a question.

"I wonder if you could help? To save me struggling to find my glasses, could you please tell me what type of loaf that is? I can't read the description from here." Seeing the embarrassed shoulder hunched titters, I'd think, 'What was so flaming funny about that? Bring back those Polish girls. Quick, lithe and efficient.'

Oh and those screaming kids. Call me old fashioned, but years back, if your mum said, "Now you can just stop that nonsense, or I'll give you something to yell about," you listened. Nowadays a parent would get locked up and child taken into care at such a common-sense approach, leaving us to endure insufferable behaviour and a parent whining, "Now stop it Timmy. You know that's not nice. Now what have you been told? You shouldn't kick peoples' doggies."

Meanwhile all those, round about are praying, "Go on pooch, bite the little bastard!"

I'm sorry. I shouldn't have gone on, but all the niggles of life became magnified with Helena gone. I prayed she'd phone, asking me to join her somewhere. A helter-skelter life as in those nighttime wild escapades. I'd be gone like a shot.

I had many abiding memories and often it was just simple occurrences that seemed so poignant. We had been out to an afternoon garden gathering and as an insufferable bore puffed out his chest to explain how things had been during his time working in the council offices, I happened to catch a glimpse of Helena with an expression of, 'Please, no! Spare us.' When our eyes met, we both had to leave the marquee, propping each other up, as the droning voice within left us absolutely aching with laughter.

Then there was the time when wearing her tight leather trousers, the day turned out incredibly hot. A real scorcher. We were driving along a fairly open road and she said wriggling, "I'm too hot in these things. Do you mind if I pull them down?"

Well of course I didn't, nor did the truck driver we overtook. Helena, did offer a covering hand in her state of reclination, but even so, looking in my rearview mirror, I was able to comment, "Well, you certainly turned his lights on."

Now she was gone and it was back to the empty house. Worse than that, I now had to contemplate the seemingly impossible. If she could survive on no food and was consuming enough electricity to charge an electric vehicle, was she actually a person?

My mind would say, 'Ridiculous,' but around it went in the same loop to conclude it was the only possible solution.

My level headed daughter, was the first to hear, what sounded increasingly absurd as I tried to explain. Although agreeing with the logic and the fact that A1 technology had become mind-blowingly clever of late, as far she could make out, actual robots were still awkward, clunky things that hardly resembled an actual being.

This came as a massive relief and then when Joe and my son confirmed, no robot had yet been constructed to rival the proverbial dream girl, I concluded there must be another solution.

Chapter Eighteen

Time dragged by, as it does in such circumstances and I had almost given up hope of hearing from Helena again, until one evening, when my whole body jerked at hearing her phone ringing. It wasn't the usual bleep, bleep, but the same sound as heard in the woods all that time back. As said, it shocked me and felt quite eerie, reminding me of that first strange encounter and leaving me wondering, how had she managed to change the ringtone?

Very cautiously I pressed the green button and said, "Hello, Helena?"

"Hello darling. Sorry it's been so long. You couldn't be a love could you and set up the phone as you did before?"

With hands shaking, I managed to activate the thing and propping it with a book on the chest of drawers, I sat on the bed and waited.

I watched with heart pounding, as the needle of light pierced, before expanding, to suddenly balloon up as Helena, standing as large as life, directly in front of me.

"Helena, I'd almost given up. You can't believe how fantastic this feels."

"I'm sorry darling, it's been so difficult. You can't believe how much we've had to clear up. My people don't like loose ends."

"But what's happened? You look so different."

"Oh, you mean these?" Her arms were folded and a quick hoist and quiver, disturbed weighty appendages slung hidden beneath the lacy decolletage.

"Well of course," I said, "and forgive me for being so personal, but you must have gone up at least two bra sizes." 'And the rest,' I thought.

"Yes, we ladies have ways of managing such things."

'Not without medical help, I shouldn't wonder,' was an observation I kept to myself.

"But do you like them?"

"Well of course, but you didn't have to do it on my account, Helena. I've always loved you just the way you are."

"Oh, that's so sweet."

There was that dreadful word, sweet, again and even though I'd not exactly gone barmy over the new double D's or whatever size they were, I'd found it devilishly difficult to look her in the eye when talking.

"So what have you been up to?"

I gave a quick rundown, including details of the police officer calling. She found my account hilarious, which was that infectious, I found myself laughing and prattling away to an ingenious ray of light as if Helena was actually there in the room with me.

Of course, I didn't mention my sky-high electricity bill, nor what I'd found out about her little white pills. I'd only just got her back and certainly didn't fancy the risk of losing her. I concentrated more on what I'd recently found so frustrating, when dealing with what used to be mere everyday tasks. I fumed, that the more infuriatingly smart society was becoming, the more difficult it seemed to get even simple things done.

Suddenly she said, "Would you like to leave all this nonsense behind. Would you like to come with me?"

"Of course, Helena, but where to?"

"I can't really tell you, but would you? Would you come with me?"

"Like a shot."

"I can't tell you any more at the moment and I have to go now. But keep the phone by you, I'll be back soon." Blowing me a kiss she breathed, "Goodnight darling."

I found myself alone, heart pounding, in the dark. I got up, paced the room, sat down, then got up again. I should have felt elated, but couldn't shake off a nagging doubt. There was something troubling, but I couldn't pin down exactly what.

Suddenly it hit me; even though she'd been bubbly, even quite girly, I'd detected a hint of desperation. It brought a sadness, that tainted what had been my absolute headlong plunge into love. Then came the question, why the cosmetic surgery? Yes, they drew the eye, but knowing what I did, there was no escaping the fact they were fake. Poor girl. She had looked so pleased with them, and yet I'd experienced an unwanted rise of pity. That was it, just as I'd felt on a previous occasion, she was trying too hard. Plus, if truly on a clandestine diplomatic mission, the last thing you'd want, unless setting a honey trap, was a pair of whoppers.

Sitting back down on the bed, I listed the words again, those words imagined when attempting to explain my demise; sadness, pity, false. Then it hit me! Of course! The whole thing was false. I didn't know how or why, but it had to be the only explanation.

So, I asked myself, would I still drop everything and go with her? Even if having fallen in love with a machine, would I still succumb?

Must admit, I didn't find it hard to reason such justifications as, 'Perhaps things would work out.' Or, 'Perhaps I'd just imagined Helena's slight sense of desperation.' Then with head in hands, I groaned inwardly, knowing she had become like a drug, almost impossible to resist.

My son, John, was the first to hear the latest and was so obviously concerned, I had to assure him I'd not be going anywhere without telling him. He'd never met Helena of course, but instincts told him, grave danger lay ahead.

My daughter, Hannah, said both she and her brother wanted me to be happy, but looking at it from a woman's point of view, felt certain, this lady Helena was up to something. She didn't quite know what, but definitely sensed an inner alarm bell ringing. "You mark my words, dad. She's a bit of a dirty one."

When I rang my friend Joe, he suggested we take that short break we'd spoken of.

It was a hotel in a charming little time warp on the Welsh Marches. I did the driving, collecting him Saturday morning and near the destination, we stopped at a castle to take a ramble over the mound it commanded. There was a tea-room down by the river, where we partook of the simple fare, coffee with homemade carrot cake and basically, just talked about this and that, plus of course old times. It wasn't until reaching the hotel, that the conversation turned to my recent dilemma.

It was still too early for dinner and so having dropped off our bags, we went down to the bar for a drink. Only taking it steady, as we'd be drinking wine later and Joe said, "Yes, and you want to stick to those halves. Remember that time you went wandering when we were in Germany. You went looking for a flaming bathroom when we had one ensuite."

I must admit, the alcohol had caused a fair deal of confusion on that particular night, meaning I'd not been able to remember our room number, but where I found myself the following morning, is a story for another time.

We at last broached the subject of lady Helena, as Hannah called her.

"Now look," said Joe, "You know me and my logical scepticism. I actually think this android notion of yours is a load of old bollocks, but let's just play along with it for a while and see where it leads."

Discussing the matter lasted through our stay in the bar, plus right through starter and main course and so I'd best just give a summary.

Joe's reasoning was, if Helena was truly a robot, then she wouldn't actually be in control. Whoever owned her would be. She was an expensive piece of kit and so couldn't be left to just wander about where the fancy took her. Therefore, he concluded, my discovery of the phone in the woods would not have been pure chance, I must have been set up.

"But why?"

"I told you, she's after your old age pension, mate."

We both laughed and then Joe surmised, "Let's just say, she *is* cutting edge A1 technology. It would mean she could do thousands of calculations in seconds and the advanced maths I sometimes struggled with, would be nothing more than child's play. But if this Helena is being passed off as just another human, she'd have to keep this amazing ability under wraps. What she would need is an infusion of the sort of everyday banter we chuck back and forth. The sort of wit we don't even have to think about."

We ordered a second bottle of wine and even though Joe was having beef and I'd chosen the lamb, we still stuck to white. Who gives a damn about convention. It's what you prefer that counts.

Joe asked, "Did you say, her face sometimes flickers when a question is thrown at her?"

"It's not a flicker as such, more like a momentary freeze. Lasts no more than a split second."

"Sounds like she's resetting herself."

We had covered the strange hologram appearances, her amazing range of knowledge, plus the fact dogs didn't like her, to the point we'd had to avoid them at all costs, but strangely cats did and then Joe asked again about Helena's shunning of food.

"You say, you've only witnessed her eating cereal and soup."

"That's right and alcohol seems to have no effect on her."

"Well, when you think about it, it wouldn't. A robot would have a little chamber somewhere that could easily be emptied and swilled out. There's probably another for food, but why have the problem of grease and possibly stinky stuff if you don't have to?"

"Sounds like you're coming around to my way of thinking. I'm a silly old duffer who's fallen for a robot."

"Not a bit of it. Silly old duffer, I'll grant you."

We both laughed and then he asked about the strange night flights again.

"How does it actually feel?"

"Like I said, frightening but exhilarating."

"Yes I know that, but what I mean is, do you feel like some sort of superman with Lois Lane by your side-------?

"No it's as if we've become one."

"So your minds seem joined?"

"Exactly and at times it brings an ecstatic feeling I can't describe."

"A Micky Finn, mate, just like I said before. I tell you what though----." He paused, then said, "Now you know I don't consider this plausible, but let's play it out a bit further. If she's truly like a drug, then you want to be careful. What it means is, you're no longer in charge of your actions. Just like a druggy. They know the needle will eventually kill them, but are unable to stop."

This home truth hit like an Exocet. It summed up my reaction when Helena had last called. I'd felt unable to resist her.

"So, tell me Joe," I said at last. "We come back to that same question, why me?"

"I suppose you're giving her, or should I say, supplying her handler, with what they can't really programme. You've led a fairly colourful life, had all sorts of experiences, can sometimes be annoyingly witty and as far as I know, there isn't a programme that simulates that. She's feeding off your mind, mate."

"And the boob job?"

"Doubt it would have been her idea. It's what her handler feels will make her irresistible."

"So you do think I've become ensnared by some sort of android."

"No, load of old bollocks, but it's been fun exploring the hypothesis. Have you got any pictures, by the way?"

We both laughed.

The next day, we had a stroll around the town, followed by a trip out to a small stone circle and late afternoon I dropped Joe off at his home in the Midlands. My dark empty house awaited.

Chapter Nineteen

It was a few days later, that I heard an unexpected knock on the door. A man with a pleasant countenance introduced himself as a policeman. He said he needed to talk to me, but if I would please oblige, he preferred discussing the matter in his car.

It seemed extremely odd, but slinging on a jacket and locking my front door, I followed him.

Sitting in the driver's seat, he said, smiling broadly, "You probably noticed on the ID I showed you, my name is Watson, but before you ask, it happens to be Detective Inspector Watson, not Dr Watson and furthermore, my boss isn't called Holmes."

I laughed, immediately taking to the man.

He asked me about Helena, just briefly, that is and then reaching behind for a folder, produced three photographs.

"Is that who you refer to as Helena?"

"Yes. They're a bit blurred, but it's definitely her. I don't understand. How did you get these?"

"They are shots taken by the casinos that banned her."

"For what?"

"Taking them to the cleaners basically. She has an uncanny ability to remember card sequences."

"That's hardly a crime."

"No, but this is."

He showed me two further photographs. The first was of, what I took to be a corpse, curled up with hands clutching his groin and the second was the close-up of a gaping red wound.

"That's horrible. What is it?"

"Where his genitals should be. He was a convicted rapist and unfortunately for him, once out and about again, picked on the wrong woman."

"Helena? How do you know?"

He sighed. "There's a fair bit we need to go through. It seems daft trying to sort it out here. Is there somewhere comfortable we could go? Coffee, cake, something like that."

"I could easily put the kettle on."

"Thank you, but it would be better if we discuss this somewhere neutral."

"There's the Royal."

"You'll have to guide me there. It's my first visit." Then turning to look me straight in the eye, he said, "Now look. Before we go any further and sorry to be tiresome, but can I ask you once again, whether this lady left anything behind in the house? It doesn't matter how insignificant it might seem."

"No nothing."

"So how does she contact you?"

"I have my phone----"

"And?" He carried on staring. Staring in that penetrating way people have when not believing you.

"She made me promise not to show it to anyone."

"She left you an electronic device."

"Yes."

"Do you have it on you?"

"No. It's in the house."

"Obviously, I understand you don't want to break her trust, but could you please go and get it."

I did and when examining it, turning it over slowly, he finally gave it a slight clench as if in triumph, before handing it back.

As mentioned in that flying extravaganza, I don't know how Helena knew it, but the new one-way system, did in fact mean a circuit of the town was required to access the only opening to the car park of the Royal Hotel. As we approached the junction, I pointed this out.

Seeing no cars queuing at the lights to our right, DI Watson exited College Street and reversing at speed past the Royal Hotel, drove into the car park and swinging us into a vacant space, completed the manoeuvre with a graunch of the hand break.

"Not a word," he said, grabbing his briefcase.

We ordered coffee along with apricot croissants and found a comfy place to sit.

He opened the main flap of his briefcase and withdrew a laptop. Flicking through contents, he finally budged his chair closer so I could see the screen. There was a series of five photographs, similar in the fact they were all of men, with hands to their heads, lying in the foetal position.

He went through them again, explaining, "This one was a retired judge. This one, a retired headmaster. A retired financial adviser; a faded 1980's pop artist and finally a retired businessman."

"But what has this got to do with Helena? Surely you're not saying she killed them."

"I'm not assuming anything. My job is to investigate. There is nothing connecting these men, other than they all enjoyed walking and died unexpectedly in fairly remote locations. They lived miles from one another, Cornwall, Wales, East Anglia-----. Their deaths would have gone unconnected, but for one thing."

"What exactly?"

"I'm sorry. I can't divulge that at the moment. It was one of our lads browsing through suspicious deaths data, who made the connection and the case was handed to me."

"Where are you based, by the way?"

"I sort of float."

"So what brought you to my door?"

"These five men, who died so unexpectedly, had all become fairly accomplished in their various fields, without ever having made national headlines. They were all fairly fit, hadn't died of heart attacks and so we have to ask, what killed them?"

"But I still don't know why this implicates Helena." Thinking for a while I said, "You mean, you found that taser story in the local paper."

"Yep! Well in fact, I didn't, one of our lads did and as we suspected each of these men could have suffered from a massive electric shock, anything involving tasers became of immense interest. We asked the local force to send details concerning, you, your lady and the Patels and voila, here I am."

Scrolling through his machine again, he brought up the CCTV photograph of myself and Helena.

I was stunned and of course, the last thing I wanted was to believe the implications. "But I still don't see how this makes Helena a possible murderess. What makes you think these men had been electrocuted?"

"I'm afraid I can't divulge that at this point, but have a look at these." Scrolling through the laptop contents again, he showed me a series of photographs, taken in various locations, pointing out, they were of the five men I'd just seen pictures of, but when very much alive. My blood ran cold, for smiling sweetly beside each of them, was Helena. Were these the liaisons she'd described, that hadn't worked out?"

DI Watson reasoned, "I'm not at this point saying she is the culprit, but I need your help. Would you let our forensics' team do a little investigation inside your house? Quite unintrusive----. No forgive me, that's nonsense. What I mean is, it will be done with respect and with any luck, they'll find hair samples."

"No need for that. I can save them the trouble, I've a hoover bunged up with the stuff."

"Fantastic. Could you let me have the contents?"

"Gladly, but why?"

"This is strictly confidential, but as your life could be at risk, you obviously need to know."

I should imagine my eyes might have widened somewhat at that point and leaning closer, I listened.

"The would-be rapist had a clump of hair in his hand and on one of the other corpses we found a strand of hair that was an exact match."

"Just one strand."

"That's all it takes."

We decided on another coffee and I of course asked, why did he think I could be a victim?

DI Watson looked slightly incredulous at this point. "You mean to say, you saw two men getting zapped by a woman who apparently was not in possession of any form of tasering device and yet you remain unnerved?"

"Of course I'm worried. After it happened, it kept me awake half the night and then to make matters worse, next day she was gone."

"How far apart were they when the one got downed in the doorway?"

"About four paces."

"And no sign of any device at all."

"No."

"So what did she do? Just point two fingers, 'Kerpow!' like a kid playing cowboys?"

"Hard to say and excuse the pun, but it all happened in a flash."

Laughing, he said, "Incredible! I'm sure we could find the likes of her a little job in the force."

The coffee arrived and leaning closer he confided, that for my sake, it was imperative he now took possession of the phone, Helena had left.

"You won't be able to get into it, it's sealed."

"Whether we can or can't, it doesn't matter. The lads will scan it. Thinking about it, it's almost certain to have a non-tamper device, so I doubt they'll even try to dismantle it."

"Don't know what good it will do. The thing only works if she rings. Then I have to press that green button."

"I just need it for a couple of days."

Reluctantly I handed it over.

We finished our coffee and after paying the bill, Detective Inspector Watson drove me home. I went inside, emptied the hoover contents into a plastic bag and returned to his car.

Taking it, he thanked me and then stressed once more, it was vital that I inform him, if Helena happened to turn up. It was also vital that she wasn't told the two of us had been in contact. Handing me a mobile phone, he said that would be our only way of contacting one another. Touching the base of the OK button brought up his number. All I then had to do, was press the button on the left with the green line. I did so and the phone in his pocket rang.

"Here's the charger and make sure you keep it fully charged. Also, don't ring me from inside the house."

I nodded and then asked, "Why all the hush-hush? Do you mean my house could be bugged?"

"No shit, Sherlock," he said with a laugh.

Exactly the same phrase as once used by Helena. Had their paths crossed along the murder trail? Or had she somehow intercepted calls of her pursuer? Returning to the house, I gave a backward glance. The police officer was still watching me, almost as if knowing there were things I'd not divulged. OK, I admit, I hadn't told him how Helena sometimes appeared in a beam of light, nor about our exhilarating night flights. Just putting it like that makes it seem ridiculous and completely implausible, so how could I have explained such phenomena to a man trained to follow the usual trail of cause and effect, crime and motive. Also, let's be truthful, I was passionately in love with Helena and couldn't imagine how our personal delights could interest the law. Simply trying to explain would sully its very beauty. Yes, I'd told Joe, but he's been a lifelong friend.

Chapter Twenty

Two days passed and I began to feel growing anxiety, for if Helena tried ringing, she'd not take kindly to her phone being in police custody. Even now, when cleaning the house, I still come across strands of her hair. I doubt a moulting cat could have left more of a statement.

In bed that night, I struggled to get to sleep, for inside was obviously a longing to see Helena again, to the extent that it hurt and yet I was also terrified, lest she discover I'd betrayed her trust. Love contrasting with dread made it almost impossible to slip into blissful repose. When I finally did, I was led through wild dreams that ended in a nightmare, almost as if Helena had entered my bedroom, to glare down at me with a face of fury.

To my horror, I realised she had.

"Where is that phone I left?" The force of her foot stamp resonated through the bell of my old alarm clock.

"Helena, incredible to see you. Why didn't you let me know? How did you get in without waking me? I honestly thought I was seeing things." Now sitting upright, with bedcovers flung back, I was ready to dash to the door if needs be. The woman I had fallen for looked absolutely terrifying.

She stood imperiously in spiteful high heels, wearing a black top of such neck-high severity, it restrained the ample bosom like a bolster, lending a matronly look.

"Never mind that," she said. "Where's that phone?"

Her tight skirt clung to just below knee length and God knock me down for it popping into my brain, but I really couldn't banish the notion and of course wouldn't have dared admit, that not only had I gone off her somewhat, but worst of all,--- standing there, almost bursting with pent up fury, she could well have been wearing grubby knickers!

What a thing to think when scared stiff and thoroughly relieved she couldn't actually read my mind, I said, "I keep it hidden."

"Not in the house, you haven't. I've scanned and can't find any trace of it."

"I'll get it for you, Helena, but please, don't you realise how dangerous it is for you here? The police have been looking for you."

"Don't make me laugh," she sneered. "It will take more than those idiots to reign me in."

"But they could be here at any minute."

The room was still pitch black, but where the curtains had not been drawn properly, I could see dawn light burgeoning. Out of the darkness, Helena's face loomed grey, mask-like and I sensed something in her manner, like a dark foreboding, as if she'd been sent on a mission. As Joe had said, it wouldn't be her in control, her handler would be. Instincts told me, I had to keep her talking.

"Helena, I know it seems ridiculous, the law siding with the robbers, rather than the robbed, but those two you zapped are still in hospital."

"They got exactly what they deserved."

"Helena, I've been told all about how you fleeced those casinos. At first I couldn't believe it. So out of character, but you took them for so much money, three have banned you."

This seemed to hit the right spot, for with a derisive laugh she said, "Like taking sweets from children."

"We could travel the world, Helena. A gambler's version of Bonny and Clyde, hitting one casino after another."

"I don't need their money. It was just a game." Then with a haughty look, "But there's no doubt you do. How are the books going, by the way?"

"I never told you about my hobby."

"You didn't need to. I know all about you; your name, which is not Daniel, of course. Pathetic!" she spat. "I know what school you went to; which University; your career and even these latest scribblings. Oh, I doubt you'll want to hear this, but in the last volume of your trilogy, you made a stupid mistake."

"Just the one? Well that's a comfort."

With a contemptuous look, "Ever the wit. Anyway, regarding the founding of present-day Padua, you wrote Prince Antenor was a Greek. He wasn't. Antenor was a Trojan prince."

"Oh, glad you found it. I just put that, so you could tell me about it."

"Very funny!"

Trying to sound as genial as possible, "And I wouldn't have described him as a Greek, Helena. The term wasn't known in 400BC."

"Don't try those diversionary tactics on me. You don't have that phone, do you?"

I shook my head.

"Let me guess. The police have it."

"I couldn't help it Helena. I was confused. They wanted anything connected to you."

"So you betrayed me."

"Not really. There's no way they can get into the thing and so I couldn't see what harm it would do. I thought if I handed it over, they would leave me alone."

"You pathetic article," she sneered.

"I'm sorry Helena. I can get it back for you. They'll probably return it today."

"Who did you give it to, exactly?"

"Just the local boys in blue."

"You're lying. Never mind any pretensions of being an author, you're like an open book!"

"They'll be bringing it back today," I said in desperation.

"Too late. Damage is already done."

I swear I'm not making this up, for as Helena raised a hand and said, "Look, I'm sorry," a tiny red dot appeared, left side of my chest and her face began to actually glow.

"Play Misty for me," I said.

In the split second, of her face freeze, I rolled off the bed to the floor. I was still completely at her mercy of course and could do nothing other than watch, but rather than come in for the kill, she stood motionless, sideways on, with face set in concentration. Then bending over me, hissed, "Consider yourself lucky I don't have a kitchen knife on me."

Helena left the room and although I pulled myself upright, it was a while before I dared follow. Creeping downstairs, I saw the front door had been left open. There was no sign of her outside and after quickly checking both downstairs rooms, I locked the front door and dared sit down. My whole body was trembling and on phoning DI Watson, using the safe phone, I could hardly get the words out. I was in such a state, I completely forgot I wasn't meant to ring him from inside the house.

"Wait there," he said. "I'll be straight round."

I went back upstairs to wash and dress and thought it best to pull the sheets and bedclothes straight. As said, it had been a torrid night and they were in disarray. On plumping up the pillow, I noticed a tiny black mark. I scraped it with a fingernail, but to no good effect and then putting on my glasses, realised it wasn't actually a mark, but a tiny hole through the pillowslip.

The phone ringing downstairs gave me a start and on descending to answer, I heard the comforting words, "I'm parked just down the street, to your right."

Donning a coat, I locked up and walked to where DI Watson was waiting. The passenger door was swung open for me to slump myself down inside.

"I'm afraid we have to hang on to your phone for a little longer," he said.

"Have you managed to discover any of its mysteries?"

"Never mind that. Tell me what happened."

My voice was still shaky, but I described as best I could, Helena's visit and then told him about the hole in the pillow.

Shaking his head in disbelief, he asked, "What ever possessed you to mention that film, 'Play Misty for Me?'"

"It was because of something my old pal, Joe told me. During a bit of banter, exploring the notion, Helena could well be a computer in human form, he said that these amazing A1 machines could calculate thousands of things per second, but weren't that hot when it comes to lateral thinking. I just thought it might throw her off for a second."

"Well machine or not, it obviously did. You can thank your mate Joe, you're still here to tell me about it."

With this, he dialled a couple of numbers and then suggested I pack an overnight bag. It was obviously not safe for me to stay in the house until the lock was changed and also forensics needed to give the place the once over.

"Have you got your mobile on you?"

"Yes."

"If you let me have it, I'll get the lads to give it the onceover."

I was driven to a house on the far side of town. The wife of the couple did secretarial work for the police and they couldn't have been kinder, had I been the lone survivor of a shipwreck. When collected, late the next day and driven home, DI Watson handed me my new keys, along with my mobile phone, saying, although it hadn't been bugged, the house had. He still preferred

I used the safe phone he'd given me, when ringing him and stressed once again, if Helena made another appearance or even just rang, it was imperative I get hold of him immediately. He also asked for contact details of my son and daughter. I would now be blessed with a trinity of guardian angels.

Chapter Twenty-One

Two days dragged by and each evening, to make sure I was alright, my daughter rang. She told me, the nice policeman had given her his mobile phone number. My son rang once, saying he was away on business, but would be back by midweek.

On the third evening, just as the street lights were coming on, my mobile rang. It was Helena.

I had been busy writing an email, but sending it into drafts, listened to her frantic whispers. She sounded terrified.

"Thank God I've got hold of you. I'm desperate. I need your help. If they find I've gone, I'm finished. I tried ringing a number of times. Why didn't you answer?"

"I thought I'd explained."

"Not to me you didn't."

"Yes I did."

"No darling----"

"Helena I did! Four nights ago you tried to kill me!"

"That wasn't me, darling. I couldn't do that. It was her. You know the person I am. How could I possibly do a thing so monstrous? My phone----where is it? What happened to it? I couldn't reach you."

"Helena, we're going round in circles."

"Do you have it?"

"Yes, I do now," I lied. "But it was you Helena, as large as life. You tried to kill me."

"It was not me, darling. Not me. Can't you understand. Look, it's too complicated to explain at the moment. I haven't much time. Can you please come to me? Please?"

"Where are you?"

"Where you first found my phone."

I could almost hear Joe's voice again, 'You were set up, mate.'

"Helena, as much as I'd like to help you, I can't right now."

"Please, you must. I'm desperate. Look, I've never said this to any man before, but I love you. You're different to any other I've ever met."

"But Helena--------"

"Please darling. And you do have that phone, don't you?"

"Yes," I lied again.

"Could you at least bring it to me?" She started to laugh, "Do you remember those fun times we had? It was like we'd known each other all our lives. Oh, I do miss you."

"I miss you too, more than you'll ever know. It's that bad, it hurts, like a deep burning."

"So will you come to me? Please say you will. Go on, say it."

Just then, my laptop screen flickered. The fact a message had been sent, was flagged up, bottom right-hand corner. I clicked on the little blue envelope and saw it was from Joe. Typical! It was a picture of a robot, looking more like a large insect, rather than human and beneath was the message, 'Load of old bollocks, mate.'

It brought me to my senses and an idea flashed, inspiring me to ask, "Helena? Tell me. Who won the FA cup in 1932?"

"**What**? This is sick! You're joking!"

"No I'm not. I need to know."

"It was what they called, the 'over the line final.' Newcastle beat Arsenal, 2-1. Now for God's sake be sensible."

The answer had been that instant, it had to have come directly from her. "Helena. That night we attended the quiz-party, do you remember it?"

"Of course, my sweet, but why?"

"You didn't receive the answers on your phone, did you?"

"What is this? What are you implying?"

"It hurts me to say it, but the answers weren't via your phone, they came directly from you."

"No, you mustn't say this! It's hateful. Can't you understand what you are doing? This will ruin everything."

Steeling myself and almost feeling I was stabbing my own heart, "Helena------"

"Stop it!! Stop it! I won't listen!"

"Helena, I know the truth." After a huge pause, with my heart pumping, I dared blurt, "Helena, as much as I love you, you are not human. You are a machine."

"How can you say this? How can you drive a stake through my heart. Can a machine cry?"

It was heart-rending, for I could hear uncontrollable sobbing at the other end.

Sounding completely distraught, "Don't you realise what you did for me? You've made me human. I'm so different to the person you first met. I thought we'd created a miracle, but now this. We were so close to defying the whole world and now you've ruined it."

"That other Helena? Are you saying, you are now two different people?"

"Yes, my darling. That's what I tried to tell you. I've broken free. But they'll destroy me unless I-----. Please come to me, darling. We are perfect for one another. We both know that. We will be as free as birds." Laughing, she added, "I can take you flying again."

"Where to, exactly?"

"Straight through that hole in the clouds. You're different to anyone I've ever met. You've done so much for me. I love you, completely and utterly----. Do you remember those lovely times we had, just sitting there, virtually naked and simply talking." With a giggle, she added, "The suspension of us being so close and yet able to resist taking the plunge, was sometimes almost unbearable. A beautiful torment that was quite innocent and unbelievably thrilling."

"Of course I remember. No other woman has ever done that for me."

"You have taught me so much. That time before, when it must have seemed like watching a video, I knew I'd made a mistake. Too much too soon. You didn't realise, but it showed on your face. And then of course, there was that small matter of breast enhancement. Obviously not a good idea."

"I have to admit, Helena, I was a bit taken aback. I'm not saying a well-endowed lady doesn't excite, but as long as that first spark of attraction lasts, it's actually the person that matters; not the Botox or appendages. I fell in love with you, Helena, for just who you are."

"Now you're making me cry again. Please say you will come to me."

"What about my children?"

"You'll still be able to contact them. Will you say yes? Go on say it."

"I'll need a little time to pack a bag."

"Oh, you darling."

"I'll be with you in 15 minutes."

"I'll be waiting. Make sure you have my phone with you."

Can you believe it, even at my age, as I rammed things into a small suitcase, my whole body shook. Then what about money? Stupid of me, I'd not be needing any. What about the phone? I obviously didn't have it, but If she truly loved me, that would hardly matter. I was in a complete dither and nearly tripped on the stairs, hurrying back to the bathroom for shaving kit and toothbrush.

I knew I was going against every ounce of common sense, in fact my very nature, but somehow couldn't help myself. In the doorway, giving one last backward glance, I thought, 'I'm coming to you my love,' and was just about to switch my phone off to put me beyond reach, when I noticed the glow of a lamp left on in the front room. Out of habit and even though I'd probably never be paying another electricity bill, I returned to switch it off.

As I did so, my mobile rang. It was Hannah.

"Hello, Han. Sorry, can't talk now, I'm in a bit of a rush."

"I thought you sounded rather breathless. Dad? What exactly are you doing?"

"It's Helena. She's desperate."

"DAD, NO! Are you listening to me?"

"Yes."

"You are not to go anywhere near her."

"But you don't understand, she's so different. It's like, everything I ever wanted."

"In what way?"

"She loves me."

"Oh my God! And did she say, you're the first man she's ever said that to?"

"Well, yes."

"And that she's never met anyone like you before? Oh, dad, you have to listen to me. That thing is evil."

"No, Hannah, she's explained it all to me."

"Are you still in the house?"

"Yes."

"Then sit down. Are you sitting down?"

"Yes, Han."

"Now don't you dare move!"

The call ended and a couple of minutes later my phone rang again. "Dad? He's on his way. He'll be with you in ten minutes. Now promise me, you'll wait for him."

"I promise, Hannah."

"And if that woman rings again, don't you dare answer."

Feeling more in control of my faculties, I thanked her and waited for the arrival of Detective Inspector Watson. My phone did ring again and I could see it was Helena calling, but I just stared at the name glowing. Thank God, somehow, the spell had been broken.

There was a knock on the door and DI Watson appeared. "You, OK?" he asked.

"Just about."

He scrolled up a number on his phone and spoke into it, "It's alright Hannah, I'm with him now. Like a word?"

Hannah could hardly talk for crying. In the end she gasped, "I've been worried sick, dad. I'm so glad you're safe."

DI Watson hovered patiently until the call ended and then said, "Excuse me for asking, but do you happen to possess a broom?"

I looked at him dumbfounded.

"You know," he said. "Just an ordinary broom."

"Yes, I have an ancient thing in the pantry. Needs chucking out, but I hadn't the heart."

We went through to the kitchen and producing the broom from the cupboard, I said, "I'm afraid it's rather elementary, my dear Watson."

Looking at the stumpy bristles, he rejoined with a smile, "No shit, Sherlock."

It must have been the pressure I'd been under, for I burst out laughing and we held our aching sides, trying to suppress the convulsions, like two kids in school assembly.

Once in control again, we headed for the front door and that's exactly how Detective Inspector Watson and myself happened to be heading for a confrontation with the most sophisticated A1 intelligence yet known to man, armed with a broom.

Well, that was my take on it. Obviously, DI Watson held more prosaic beliefs, following clues and crime trails, misdeeds and motives, but even so, he still requested precise details of our destination, to radio in for back-up.

Chapter Twenty-Two

We parked near the woods; the car being lit by the eerie light cast by the final lamppost before the enclave of wilderness beyond. Opening the car boot, Inspector Watson produced a black bag.

"What exactly is that?" I asked.

"That phone you gave me. Have you got the broom?" Seeing me brandish it he said, "Then come on!"

I led the way and we topped the small rise to the right of the main path. Once in the clearing he quietly asked, "Is this it?"

I nodded and lowering the bag, he opened it. Using the broom handle, the phone was prodded out onto the grass. "Now we wait," he whispered.

An owl hoot enhanced the drama and as if taking this as a cue, the phone rang.

"Step back," Watson instructed and reaching out, gave the green button on the phone a tentative prod with the broom handle.

Being ripped from his grasp, the cleaning utensil flew clear across open ground, to clatter against the trees.

"Holy Mother," he said, ruefully rubbing his right hand. Shortly after, we watched as the phone began to crackle, then burst into flames.

"What I couldn't tell you before," he murmured, "at all five murder sites we found a small incinerated pile of debris." Then, putting a friendly arm around my shoulder, he said, "Now come on, enough excitement, we'll leave it for the local lads and forensics to clear up."

As we descended to the path, figures emerged as if from nowhere, some in uniform, others in coverall white suits. After exchanging words with a plain-clothes officer, he led the way to the car.

Police vehicles were parked everywhere, but enough room had been left to reverse out and once back in the gloominess of my house, DI Watson informed me, the DNA from the hair sample I'd provided matched exactly what they had on record. They had also found cat hair.

"The neighbour's cat would sometimes creep in to lie on Helena's bed."

"I think you mean, your bed," was said in that candid manner, experienced lawyers and lawmen tend to have.

I thought it would be best to inform him of the strange circular indentation I'd seen in the clearing we'd visited and he said they'd come across similar at two of the murder sites.

"What on earth was that black bag, you carried the phone in?"

"Anti-explosive. That thing was lethal. We couldn't possibly have let you have it back again?"

"What did they discover when they scanned it?"

"I'm afraid I'm not allowed to divulge that. What I can tell you, mind you, is it rang a few times, which rather put the wind up them and the profile of the contents matched exactly, the molten remains at those other five sites."

"So mine would have been the sixth."

"Afraid so."

"But why?"

As he rose to leave, he said, "It's difficult to say at this point, but perhaps you'd served your purpose."

His words sent ice through my veins, for Helena herself had said, 'Her people didn't like loose ends.' But who were her people? Plus how could she have sounded so convincing, when saying she loved me? I know I'd finally managed to resist the siren's call, but even so, I knew deep down I still loved her. That feeling would linger for a long time and the fact I'd never before had such an instant and deep relationship, was burnt deep inside like a scar. It had hurt like you wouldn't believe, telling her I knew the truth. So what beats me is, how could she have even countenanced the thought of my death being on her conscience?

I answered my own question; 'Perhaps she doesn't have a conscience. If she truly was a machine, then she wouldn't have.' Then the thought struck me, 'Had her strange disappearances been in order to bring other machines like herself, up to speed? And what if the next stage of this weird A1 business, did manage to incorporate the semblance of a conscience? Or even a soul?'

'Then look out civilisation,' I thought. 'We wouldn't be able to differentiate between androids and people and with them being a far superior species, they would either enslave us, or wipe us out. If wealthy Greeks in their glory days could consider slaves, nothing more than possessions that happened to breathe, then it wasn't hard to imagine machines thinking likewise.'

So where was Helena from? Perhaps an astrologer could devise the answer. I doubted an astronomer could.

Chapter Twenty-Three

So here I sit, typing my strange tale. On my children's advice, I sold the house and slipped my moorings to live in foreign parts. My money goes a lot further, the weather is better, things actually work here and there is none of that woke nonsense.

Detective Inspector Watson kept in contact, saying no trace of Helena having worked for the foreign office or diplomatic corps had been found. The two thieves, she'd tasered had finally left hospital. Forensics still couldn't say for definite, what had made the circular indentation in the clearing and they couldn't find any match for Helena's hair-type on their database.

He said, "It's quite baffling. In fact, the nearest match they'd found was from a---"

"A cat," I posited. He had sounded truly stunned.

So, I'm acclimatising to my new life. The people are friendly, without being too in your face; and you'll like this bit; wine equal to a £14 bottle in England, is roughly £2 a litre.

Oh, I see, I've just had an email. That's strange, it's titled, Happy Valentine and we're nowhere near February. There's no message beneath, just a You Tube link, which can hardly hurt to open. Pity you can't hear it. It's Roberta

Flack singing that haunting ballad, 'The first time ever I saw your face.'

One of those timeless songs. Believe me, it has not lost its magic; simply beautiful. In fact, I remember it being used on the sound track of a film, way back in the 70's. Can't remember the title. It'll come to me in a minute.

Well, I could look it up of course. No I'll leave you to do that, for there's someone at the door--------

Other works by the Author

"It's all part of the game." A story based on 30 years in the antiques trade.

"The Teller." A trilogy set in the Bronze and Iron Ages.

All four books, published by Grosvenor House Publishing.

9 781803 818290